Taking Wing

by Nancy Price Graff

Clarion Books   New York

Clarion Books
a Houghton Mifflin Company imprint
215 Park Avenue South, New York, NY 10003
Copyright © 2005 by Nancy Price Graff

The text was set in 11-point Baskerville Book.

www.houghtonmifflinbooks.com

Printed in the U.S.A.

Library of Congress Cataloging-in-Publication Data
Graff, Nancy Price, 1953–
Taking wing / by Nancy Price Graff.
p. cm.
Summary: With his father in the Army Air Corps and his mother
diagnosed with tuberculosis, thirteen-year-old Gus sets out to incubate
a nest of orphaned duck eggs on his grandparents' farm in Vermont.
ISBN 0-618-53591-8
1. World War, 1939–1945–United States–Juvenile fiction. [1. World War,
1939–1945–United States–Fiction. 2. Orphaned animals–Fiction.
3. Ducks–Fiction. 4. Farm life–Vermont–Fiction. 5. Vermont–Fiction.
6. Grandparents–Fiction.] I. Title.
PZ7.G75158Tak 2005
[Fic]–dc22
2004021339

ISBN-13: 978-0-618-53591-0
ISBN-10: 0-618-53591-8

VB   10   9 8   7   6   5   4   3   2   1

To Chris, with love, for always being there,
and to Ray, who was there when I needed him

Chapter One

Gus was sitting on a wobbly stool behind his grandparents' old white farmhouse, shelling peas under a blistering June sun, when he heard his grandfather's voice rising like a storm. The dull throbbing of the tractor, which had been droning on for more than an hour like some large annoying insect, had suddenly died. Now the air was filled with a silence that seemed more empty than quiet. All he could hear was his grandfather.

"Lily! Lily! Damn it all, Lily!"

The way the voice was growing in strength, like thunder approaching over the Vermont hills, Gus knew his grandfather was coming up from the edge of the pond, where he'd been haying. And Gus knew he was moving fast for an old man with aching knees. He stood up quickly, knocking the stool to the ground behind him. He lay the bowl of shelled peas in the grass, careful not to spill the fruit of his morning's tedious labor. Then he headed toward the front of the house to see what all the commotion was about.

"Lily! For Pete's sake, damn it! Damn it all!"

Gus turned the corner just as his grandfather reached the road, a thin brown line that separated the farmhouse from the green fields and pond that lay beyond. His grandmother appeared at the front doorway.

"August, what is it? What in heaven's name has got you so riled?" His grandmother's normally soft voice was higher and louder than usual, though whether she was irritated or alarmed, Gus couldn't tell. She took a step down onto the first of the three massive granite blocks that served as the stoop and plucked nervously at her flowered apron where the ruffled straps started to run up over her shoulders.

Gus's grandfather stopped abruptly. A cloud of bone-dry dust bloomed from the roadbed and swirled around his work boots.

"A duck. A damn duck," he sputtered. He swept off his straw hat with one hand and beat it against his leg so vigorously that dirt and grass flew from the knees of his faded overalls. Then he bent over and put his rough, massive hands on his knees. On the top of his head, away from the gray fringes that lined his weathered face, his hair was still red. Looking at him bent over in the road trying to catch his breath, Gus was reminded afresh how he came by his own red hair and fair coloring, complete with freckles.

"What's all this gibberish about a duck?" Gus's grandmother demanded, now sounding as ornery as an angry wasp. She hurried over the small patch of front lawn to her husband and laid a hand on his back. Then she bent her white head beside his and looked up at him, her eyes full of concern. "August, don't frighten me! Are you or are you not all right?"

"Yes, yes." His grandfather sighed, gaining his breath and straightening up with effort. His round face was still red, but his breathing was coming more regularly. He put his hand on his wife's broad shoulder to steady himself. "I'm fine, Lily. I'm just winded, that's all. But tarnation, I killed a duck!"

"Is that what this foolishness is about?" Gus's grandmother asked. "You just about do yourself in running up the hill and make a ruckus that gives me palpitations, all because you killed a duck?"

"How'd you kill it?" Gus asked, edging closer.

"It was nesting. Down by the pond. I didn't see it in the tall grass, and when I did, it was too late," his grandfather said, looking the way you'd expect a man to look who a moment before had murdered an innocent animal after a lifetime of raising them.

"Why didn't it just get out of the way?" Gus asked. He couldn't imagine why anything wouldn't move if it saw a tractor bearing down on it. Tractors were big green machines that belched smoke. They had grilles and headlights that gave them menacing, maniacal smiles and pop eyes to match, like a grasshopper that had never stopped growing. Plus he could personally testify that tractors made a fearsome, deafening noise up close. When his grandfather let him ride on his, Gus bracing himself behind the scalloped iron seat, the tractor filled his head with so much noise, you would have thought that Gideon himself was blowing his trumpet smack in your ear. It made his head hurt just to think.

"She was sitting on her nest," Gus's grandfather explained, his face slowly resuming its normal sunburned color and looking less like a ripe cherry.

"So?" Gus asked. To him, that didn't change anything about how scary the tractor would have been, especially to something as small as a duck.

"She must have been trying to protect her eggs," Gus's grandmother said. "No mother wants to lose her babies. She'll do anything to protect them."

"Even die?" Gus asked.

"Even die," his grandfather said. "And the biggest shame is that I only broke one egg. If she'd flown off for less than a minute and come back, she'd still have almost her whole clutch. That's the pity."

"It's not your fault, August," Gus's grandmother said, reaching up and patting his cheek as though he were a five-year-old who had skinned his knee.

"No, but I killed her all the same."

"What about the eggs?" Gus asked.

"They'll die now, too, Gus," his grandfather said. "Without her, they can't make it."

"Come inside, August," Gus's grandmother said, taking her husband's hand and leading him into the shade of the maple trees in the front yard and toward the door.

Together, the three of them went over the threshold, long since scuffed bare of paint, and down the dark, cool hallway to the kitchen at the rear of the house.

"I know sugar's scarce, but I'll make some lemonade. They don't mean for us to go completely without just because there's a war on," his grandmother said as his grandfather sank heavily into one of the kitchen chairs. He put his elbow up on the red-and-white-checked oilcloth that covered the table and laid his cheek in the cup of his palm.

"Don't take it so hard, August," his grandmother said as she bustled around the kitchen. She collected two lemons from the small white icebox and a glass pitcher from the massive oak cupboard that filled one wall. "It's not as if you meant to kill her. You didn't even know she was there. Usually, though, we know right to the day when a duck arrives."

"Still, it's the waste of it," Gus's grandfather protested. "If I'd been paying more attention, if I hadn't been daydreaming, maybe we could've had a flock of ducks on the pond this summer. That would've been nice. It's hard enough having the cows gone. I would have enjoyed watching those ducklings grow up. I would have enjoyed that very much. Now I expect the drake will take off first chance he gets, before we even see him."

Gus knew his grandfather missed the cows. Just a year earlier, when it looked as though the United States was going to enter the world war, he had up and sold off his cows. Gus couldn't believe it when he heard it.

The Amsler farm was the last farm at the end of a dirt road. It was set in a bowl, with the farmhouse and big red barn perched halfway up one side and a pond almost the size of a baseball field sunk in the center of the bowl. All around were fields and, beyond them, woods that encircled the pond and farmhouse like a Christmas wreath. His grandfather had always farmed, had always farmed *this* farm. Gus knew his grandfather had inherited it from his father, and his great-grandfather from his father before him. Who could reckon how far back this inheritance went? Probably at least to the building of this farmhouse, more than a hundred years earlier.

But finally all those frigid mornings out in the barn milking and all those scorching summer afternoons cutting hay—even if it was on a used tractor that was the envy of half the farmers in Miller's Run—had gotten to be too much. Gus's grandfather had said he was too tired to continue, what with all the young men probably going off to fight and only old men and young boys left at home to help with the chores. And Gus's father certainly didn't want the farm. Years before he'd joined the Army Air Forces to do his part in the war, he'd been lucky enough to get a scholarship to go to college, and after that he'd gotten an office job he liked in Boston.

According to Gus's grandmother, it had hurt his grandfather so much to see the last cow led away that he hadn't been able to watch. He had gone into the house, shoved his hands deep into his overall pockets, and stared out the back kitchen window, though what exactly he was looking at, she couldn't say.

Now these green hillsides were bare of sweet brown cows, whose eyes were so soft and liquid they had reminded Gus of chocolate milk. But Gus's grandfather still mowed the fields—just to keep up appearances, he told everyone—and these days he gave the hay away to neighboring farmers who came up short in their own fields. The only animals he had left were a dozen noisy chickens, which really belonged to Gus's grandmother, one big pig—a huge, snorting sow that lived in a pen off the side of the barn—and her litter of squealing piglets, which, taken all together, didn't amount to a hill of beans.

"Why don't we raise the ducks, Grandpa?" Gus asked.

His grandmother brought two tall glasses of lemonade to the table and put them down. Though not yet summer, the morning's heat instantly bathed the cold glasses with mist.

"It doesn't work that way, Gus," his grandfather said after taking a sip and puckering his lips. "Those eggs need a lot of attention. They need to be incubated. They need that mother duck to sit on them day and night and keep them warm until they hatch."

"But we could wrap them in something," Gus protested.

"It's more complicated than that," his grandfather countered. "Eggs are very particular. They need constant warmth. They need to be turned."

"August," Gus's grandmother said quietly, "what you're talking about is an incubator. And we have one. Don't you remember? We bought it for my chickens one year."

"Oh, Lily," Gus's grandfather said, waving his hand at her as if she were a fly loose in the kitchen. "That was ages ago. It probably doesn't work anymore. I don't believe I could even find it."

"It must be out in the barn," Gus's grandmother continued without pause, as if she could no more see her husband's hand waving in the air than lay an egg herself. "Heaven knows, everything's out in the barn somewhere."

"It wouldn't work," Gus's grandfather insisted. "Even if I could find the incubator and make it work, it wouldn't work."

"What wouldn't?" Gus asked.

"Trying to incubate those eggs," his grandfather said.

"But *why* wouldn't it work?" Gus persisted.

"It's just a silly, sentimental notion to think we could hatch those eggs," Gus's grandfather said.

"I think you need to think of Gus," said his grandmother. She tilted her head in her grandson's direction. "It may not be your fault that the duck is dead, but it's not his fault either that he's here for the summer, maybe longer. He needs something, August. It's going to be a long summer on a farm for a thirteen-year-old boy accustomed to city ways and city things. He could use something to occupy him."

"Lily, I think it's a terrible idea," Gus's grandfather said. "And what if, against all odds, the eggs hatch? Then what?"

"Then we'll cross that bridge." Gus's grandmother said. "We won't invent trouble. We'll just deal with whatever comes along, same as we always have."

"Please, Grandpa," Gus begged.

Even before his grandmother had expressed it, Gus had had the same thought about the summer in Vermont. His dad was somewhere on an Army Air Force base in Texas. And his mother? Well, that was a longer story. After coughing for six months and losing so much weight that she looked as hard and thin as a pencil, his mother had promised his dad to go to the doctor after Gus's father left. The doctor told her she had caught tuberculosis somewhere, maybe in the school where she volunteered three mornings a week, and needed at least six months of complete rest. He'd sent her to a sanatorium in upstate New York, where she could lie bundled in a blanket on a chaise on the lawn, resting and breathing fresh mountain air with other recuperating TB patients. That left Gus. It had been his father's idea to send Gus to his grandparents' farm until his mother was well enough to go home.

Now here he was in Miller's Run, knowing no one, living at the end of a dirt road with only his grandparents, some nervous chickens, and an ornery hog for company. He'd come up barely a week before on the train, but already he was homesick, not just for his parents but also for Boston, for the noise of the traffic and the playground where all the kids in his neighborhood played kick the can every night after dinner. Gus looked at the summer ahead and imagined it as a ball of twine that had no end.

"I'm against this, Lily. I think we'll only get his hopes up and then dash them when the eggs don't hatch," Gus's grandfather said, ignoring him. He pushed himself to his feet and hobbled toward the door. "But because you think otherwise, and because I love you and respect your opinion, even when I think you're acting crazier than a cat with its tail caught in the door, I'll go out and see if I can find that old incubator. We'll be damn lucky if I find it, and luckier still if it works."

"August Amsler, you watch your language," Gus's grandmother scolded. "I forgive you for cussing when you're riled up, but now you're cussing for the sheer joy of it. That's another thing altogether."

"I'm still riled up," Gus's grandfather grumbled as he disappeared down the hallway.

Gus's grandmother turned to him. "Your grandfather thinks this is a sorry idea. You are going to have to prove him wrong," she said. "If he finds that incubator and gets it working, you and you alone will have the responsibility of caring for those eggs."

"What will I have to do?" Gus asked. His grandmother's tone of voice was casting a pall over his vision of a handful of cuddly ducklings, and he was suddenly seized with anxieties about the new job he was taking on, with all its uncertainties and unknown responsibilities.

"Right now," his grandmother said, "what you have to do is go back outside and finish shelling those peas."

Gus's fingernails were sore and green when his grandfather appeared at the back porch door half an hour later.

"The incubator's all set up," he announced. "I wouldn't have thought it would still work, but when I plugged it in, the light came on, and it seems to be heating up just fine. I got the eggs from down by the pond. Let's go put them in. Thank your lucky stars for the warm sun this morning, or those eggs would have died, for sure. Who knows, maybe they already have."

There were seven eggs, eight if you counted the one the tractor had crushed. Looking at them nestled in the basket his grandfather had used to collect them, Gus thought they looked like perfection itself. Each warm egg was slightly bigger than a chicken's egg, and soft brown, the color of damp sand tinged with pale green.

Gus's grandfather showed him how to lift each egg by scooping his whole hand underneath it so as not to accidentally crack it by squeezing it between his fingers. Gus liked the shell's texture, not perfectly smooth, like glass, but slightly coarse. It reminded him of the feel of newly washed cotton dried on the line. He liked better yet the idea that within each one was a duckling, a tiny living duck with a beating heart probably no bigger than the peas he'd been shelling all morning.

The incubator looked like something out of a science-fiction magazine, an invention man might someday use to go to the moon. It was made of wire and curved tin, with a single bare light bulb hanging down in the center. Gus half expected the contraption to take off once he had filled it with its alien cargo.

When he had all seven eggs arranged under the warm light, Gus stepped back to admire the effect.

"I forgot," his grandfather said suddenly. "Just a minute." He turned and limped over to a little shelf that was part of his work-bench and rummaged around until he found what he was look-ing for. When he returned, he handed Gus a pencil stub.

"Put an X on the side of each egg," he instructed Gus. "When you're done, turn the egg over and put a Y on the other side."

"Why?" Gus asked as he leaned over and attended to his task.

"Because you'll have to turn each egg several times a day, just like their mother would have, to keep them baking evenly," his grandfather explained. "This way you'll know if you've done your job. And while you're at it, sprinkle some water on them when you turn them. Their mother would have kept them damp with her feathers. You're their mother now. Whatever she would have done, you've got to do. I just hope you and your grandmother, bless her soul, know what you've taken on. I've been around animals all my life, but you wouldn't catch me being nursemaid to a clutch of wild duck eggs."

Gus picked up the seventh egg and scratched an *X* across the curving side while he listened to his grandfather wind down. Then he rolled the egg over and began to draw a *Y*, but the tip of the pencil suddenly pierced the delicate shell. As the egg cracked, Gus instinctively gripped it more tightly. The egg shattered in his hand, and the broken yolk slipped through his fingers and landed with a soft plop near his feet. He stared in speechless horror at the crushed shell in his hand and the slimy strings of yellow and red yolk dripping from his fingers.

"Oh, Gus, my boy," his grandfather said softly. "This could be a perilous road you're taking. I think it best if you don't tell your grandmother about this mishap." He reached into his back pocket and pulled out his handkerchief. He picked the largest pieces of shell from Gus's hand and tossed them into the nearby hay. He then gently wiped Gus's fingers.

"Those red strings are blood vessels. At least we know there's something in those eggs," his grandfather said, wadding the soiled handkerchief and shoving it back down into the pocket of his overalls.

Finally, Gus dared to look up. "I've got six more," he said hopefully.

"That you do," his grandfather said as he retreated toward the doorway, where the noonday sun was almost blinding on the trampled hay underfoot. "I believe dinner is on the table, son, and if you know your grandmother, you don't want to be late to the table."

After dinner, Gus returned to the barn to be alone with

the eggs. He poked around in the barn until he found an old tin milking pail, which he carried over beside the incubator and upended to make a seat. There he sat, with his chin in his hands and his elbows on his knees, until his back ached. He watched the eggs as if he expected the miracle of life to be played out before his very eyes. Every once in a while, he carefully turned the eggs, but nothing else happened, nothing moved or squeaked or changed in any way. The eggs lay under the warm light, as still as stones, but Gus couldn't tear himself away. Beneath those fragile shells, tiny ducks were warm and growing. He had no idea if they would hatch in two weeks or two months, or what he would do when they did.

When his grandmother called him in for supper, he was surprised to find that the afternoon had slipped past. The sun was hovering above the crowns of the trees at the top of the bowl, and the light raking through the pair of big maples in the front yard was so bright and green it startled him.

He ate the peas he had shelled, along with a slice of potted meat. He missed real meat. He hated the processed canned meat of indeterminable origins that had become standard fare since shortly after the Japanese had bombed Pearl Harbor. After that, the government had begun appropriating meat for its soldiers, leaving civilians like Gus and his grandparents hungry for a pot roast. For a moment, he thought fondly of the sow outside and her noisy brood of piglets. He also thought of his father, and hoped his dad was grateful for his son's sacrifice and all the other sacrifices people were making for the war effort.

"Don't forget to carry the slops out to the pig," his

grandmother reminded him when they stood up after supper.

Gus hated this job. The pig was frighteningly big already, and her little beady black eyes stared out at him as if she suspected him of harboring evil thoughts toward her babies. He carried the bucket carefully and poured the mixture of crusts and pea pods and sour milk over the fence into her trough so quickly that it splashed on his overalls. Great, he thought, now I'll smell like the pig.

Before he returned to the house, he went into the barn to say goodnight to the eggs. They lay undisturbed in the incubator, a halo of light shedding warmth and hope in the barn's growing darkness. Carefully he rolled each one half a turn until all the Ys were visible. Then he went over to the bucket of water his grandfather always kept in the barn in case of fire and cupped his hands and filled them. He had no idea how much water the eggs needed, so he just sprinkled it over the tops of the eggs and watched it run down through the screening beneath them.

Turning around, he became aware of a commotion down at the pond. He walked to the barn door and saw his grandfather shuffling across the grass, headed toward the road. Gus sprinted to join him. Loud quacking rent the quiet evening and echoed off the hills, but there was nothing to see. They stood in the road without saying a word and listened to the clamor.

"What's going on, Grandpa?" Gus asked. "I thought you killed the duck."

"I did kill the duck, Gus. My guess is it's the drake. He's discovered the nest is gone," Gus's grandfather said.

Just then they saw a lone duck, its iridescent head a bright green in the twilight, flying up and away from the pond, headed west.

"Yep, I'm afraid that's the last we'll see of him," Gus's grandfather said.

Before he could stop them, tears flooded Gus's eyes, and he looked away. Two months ago he had stood on the platform at South Station in Boston and said goodbye to his dad as he left for basic training. After his father had turned one last time on the train steps to blow a kiss to Gus and his mother, four people had come rushing up beside them on the platform. The younger couple had kissed quickly and whispered to each other before the man broke away and disappeared into the train. Afterward, the young woman had collapsed, sobbing, in the older woman's arms. "Mama, I'm never going to see him again. I just know it," she had wailed while the other woman patted her back.

Gus's mother had glanced down at her son taking in this scene, grabbed his hand, and, to his mortification, hustled him down the platform as if he were a three-year-old.

"She knows no such thing," his mother had said between gritted teeth as tears coursed down her own cheeks. "*Your* father *is* coming home."

Gus blinked hard and fast now, and turned back to look at the empty purpling sky. Staring hard at the spot where the drake had shrunk to a speck and then vanished, he wished he had the power to draw the drake back to the eggs and hold his family together. But the drake was just as powerless to hold his family together as Gus was. Standing there, Gus felt almost as motherless and fatherless as the eggs. Of course, he had his grandparents to love him. But love wasn't the problem; he quickly ticked off the names of the people who loved him, starting with his mother and father. The ducks had loved their children, too, he guessed. Hadn't the mother been willing to die rather than abandon her eggs? And hadn't the drake sounded distraught when he returned and found his mate dead, the eggs gone?

No, the problem wasn't lack of love. It was finding your life suddenly turned topsy-turvy and put into someone else's hands for safekeeping. Hard as it was for Gus to look across the vast sea of uncertainty before him, he knew that his grandparents had taken him in, and if things didn't work out here, his mother had said he could try living with Aunt Karen and Uncle Paul in Connecticut, even though they already had their hands full with three little girls. But the ducklings, Gus thought—they had only him. He was the only thing protecting their place in the world, the only one willing to give them a chance. And what was he? A thirteen-year-old boy who hardly knew where he himself belonged anymore.

Chapter Two

Gus heard the truck wheezing as it climbed the hill. He was mucking out the pigpen, shoveling the manure through the slats of the fence while the sow faced him menacingly from the far corner, her piglets squirming by her side. He had wanted to go to the village with his grandparents, but his grandfather had decided that cleaning up after the pigs in the barn instead might make Gus more careful about picking up after himself in the house. Now he was hot, he was tired, he could hardly breathe for the stink, and he was filthy. But he was grateful—the sow had retreated to the corner when he had arrived with his shovel, and she had stayed there, snorting like a steamroller but keeping her distance. Without taking his eyes off her, he backed up to the fence and climbed it, swinging the shovel over the top rail as he jumped to the ground on the other side. He propped the shovel against a post in the barn's cellar and hurried out to meet his grandparents.

"Yoo-hoo!" He heard his grandmother calling above the engine's rattle as the truck hit the top of the rise. "Yoo-hoo, Gus!"

Now he could see his grandmother holding her blue pill-box hat flattened to the top of her head with her left hand and waving her right arm out the passenger-side window. In her hand was a white envelope.

Gus's heart leapt. In an instant he was running. By the time his grandfather had parked the truck beside the barn, Gus was reaching for the letter with the two cleanest fingers he could find.

"Hold your horses there, son," his grandfather said as he opened his door and climbed down from the truck cab. He gave his grandson an appraising glance. "Learned your lesson?"

"Yes, sir," Gus said.

"Well, we all want to hear what your father has to say. Why don't you wash up and wait until your grandmother's had a chance to take her parcels into the house and hang up her hat."

"Oh, bother with the hat, August," his grandmother said, patting at her windblown hair. "What's your father say, Gus?"

Gus forgot about his dirty hands and ripped open the letter. He began reading aloud.

Hi ya, Buster,

I am settled into basic training at Randolph Field, near San Antonio, Texas. You wouldn't like it very much here (no green trees, no hills), but Hitler and Hirohito aren't giving us much choice in the matter, so we'll do what has to be done.

Every morning we're up at 5:50, so it feels like I'm back on the farm with the cows to milk. We have about 15 minutes to get dressed and look out the window for the neon signal rings on top of the mess hall that tell us whether we need to add raincoats or white gloves or anything else to our basic uniform. Then we hurry into formation with our cadet regiments. We have to be careful never to put our hands in our pockets, because that would be two demerits. I'll bet you can guess that's pretty hard for me, but I'm doing better.

I'm not ashamed to say I was plenty scared that first day when my flying instructor strapped me into a plane and we bounced down the runway and into the air. It's hard to imagine that God ever intended us to fly, but fly we did, by golly, and now I love it. Everything looks different from up there. We'll have to get you up there sometime when the war is over and things have calmed down a bit. I'd love to fly over the farm and dip my wings to you, but I have a lot to learn before the government is going to trust me with an airplane, and Vermont is a far piece from Texas.

Please be good and please tell Grandma and Grandpa that I am well and learning how to be a soldier.

"Heavens to Betsy," Gus's grandmother said, putting a trembling hand over her heart. "They have him up in one of those contraptions already."

"That's what he went down there to do, Lily," Gus's grandfather said. "You'd best get used to it."

Together, his grandparents lifted several paper sacks from the truck seat and headed for the house, still discussing the merits of flight.

Gus looked down at the last lines of his father's letter.

Please don't worry about your mother. She's getting good care, and the doctor says she'll be all right if she gets plenty of rest and fresh air. I miss you, Gus. Flying is exciting, but if I had my druthers, I'd be home playing catch with you.

Write when you can.

Love,
Dad

Gus carefully folded the letter, now dotted with his dirty fingerprints, and fitted it as best he could back into the torn envelope. Then he went into the barn and climbed the ladder into the mow, where hay, musty with age, billowed over the floor like ocean waves. For a while he just lay in the hay and thought about how much his life had changed in the past two months. It was enough to make his head spin. When he tried to picture his mother, all he could see were her eyes, glistening with tears and ringed with dark circles as she kissed him goodbye for who knew how long. Finally, he stood up and made his way through the hay over to where one of the rafters angled into the wall. He patted the space behind the rafter to be sure it was dry, and then laid the letter carefully in the crook of the beams, where it would be safe.

Every morning for a week, Gus got up and went out to the barn to check on the eggs before he ate breakfast. They were always the same. They lay in their soft cocoon of light, sometimes with the Xs facing up and sometimes with the Ys facing up, but otherwise indistinguishable from the eggs of the day before. He turned them gently whenever he passed the barn, and sprinkled water on them three times each day.

Even with the cows gone, Gus loved being in the barn. Three stories tall, with a small gable on top and two rows of windows running the length of it, it was full of shadows and raking light that reminded Gus of the big church he and his parents attended in Boston. He never tired of looking at the angled light, alive with dancing motes of hay and dust. The barn had an ancient ripe smell that made his nose tingle every time he came through the doorway. Tucked in the corners were pieces of old equipment, dented milk cans and wooden scythes, threshers and hay rakes, and heaven knew what else.

Whenever he could, Gus went out to the barn just to sit on the upturned pail next to the incubator. The eggs were silent, but the barn was not. Birds flitted in and out of the doorway, cooing in their nests high overhead in the beams. Occasionally, mice, fat and shiny from dining on decades of animal feed that had been spilled and forgotten, chased each other along well-worn paths. He could sometimes hear the sow grunting down below or outside in her pen, and occasionally he could hear the piglets squeal, as if they were sharing a joke.

His grandmother let him take a stack of old *Life* magazines out to the barn to help pass the time. Although he didn't dare admit it to anyone, Gus thought the war was exciting. In the parlor, in the evenings, he enjoyed lying on the floor beside his grandparents' modern radio, a big, polished wooden box fitted with tall speakers arrayed like arched cathedral windows. Like millions of other Americans, Gus and his grandparents tuned in every day to hear Edward R. Murrow, Lowell Thomas, and other overseas reporters, in their deep sonorous voices, inform their listeners of troop movements in Africa and Europe, the success of the German troops rolling across North Africa, and General MacArthur's progress in the South Pacific. Now, beside the incubator, he sat on the upturned pail and pored over the photographs in *Life*, imagining his father in a bomber wiping out entire units of invading Krauts and Japs.

"How are the eggs doing?" His grandmother asked one morning as she and Gus worked in the vegetable garden beside the house. She was a generously built woman, and her thick white hair was pulled back from her face and pinned into a knot. Leaning over was hard work for her and left her red-faced, with wisps of hair flitting about her face like flies. President Roosevelt had called on every family with a plot of dirt to have a Victory Garden and do what they could to grow their own food as part of the war effort—but as far back as Gus could remember, his grandmother had always had a large garden, Victory or not. Now he had been recruited for daily garden chores, which he and his grandmother generally undertook in the morning, before the sun climbed too high.

"They're the same, Grandma," Gus said. "When do you think they're going to hatch?"

"I haven't any idea," she said, straightening up and putting her fists in the small of her back, where her lumbago made her stiff and sore. "Or even *if*," she reminded him. "Just remember that ' "Hope" is the thing with feathers.' "

Gus looked up. "What's *that* mean?"

"It's a poem by Emily Dickinson. I learned it in school," his grandmother replied. And then she closed her eyes, as if the words were written on the inside of her eyelids and began to recite:

> "Hope" is the thing with feathers—
> That perches in the soul—
> And sings the tune without the words—
> And never stops—at all—
>
> And sweetest—in the Gale–is heard—
> And sore must be the storm—
> That could abash the little Bird
> That kept so many warm—
>
> I've heard it in the chillest land—
> And on the strangest Sea—
> Yet, never, in Extremity,
> It asked a crumb—of Me.

"I still don't get it," Gus said.

"It was Miss Dickinson's way of saying that hope sustains us all," his grandmother said.

"What's that got to do with feathers?"

"Oh, that's just her fancy language. It means that hope sits in our hearts the way a chicken sits on her nest. But in this case, your hope really *does* have feathers." His grandmother chuckled, then turned serious. "But you must prepare yourself. It's possible that nothing will come of all this. Just remember—however things turn out—what Miss Dickinson was saying is that you always carry your hope right here." With that, she patted her chest and left a smudge of dark dirt over her heart.

⸙

Ten days after Gus's grandfather had set up the incubator, Gus was growing discouraged. Sometimes he got angry at the eggs for refusing to change. He watered them, he turned them—and they lay there as senseless as stones. Maybe his grandfather had been right.

After dinner on the fourteenth day, he got up from the table and put his dishes in the sink. He still wasn't used to calling lunch "dinner," but he guessed that was just how it was in the country.

"Still turning the eggs?" his grandfather asked as he pushed himself away from the table.

"I am," Gus said, stopping in the doorway on his way to the barn.

"Any sign of hatching?"

"Nope," replied Gus. He was about ready to give up hope, with or without feathers, but admitting that to his grandfather was more than he could do.

"Well, I'm proud of you," his grandfather said, to Gus's surprise. "I thought you'd fall down on the job after a day or two and just quit. I'm proud to see you sticking with it. Shows gumption."

As Gus rounded the dooryard into the barn, he stopped short. Someone was standing over the incubator. Boy or girl, he couldn't tell. Not even man or woman, though the figure was small for a full-grown woman and smaller still for a man. The hair was dark brown, the color of a walnut, and cut lop-sided across the back, just below the ears. The seat of the overalls had been patched more than once with big, sloppy stitches his grandmother would never have tolerated, and the pant legs showed a great deal of filthy ankle and feet.

"Hey, you! What are you doing?" Gus shouted, taking several steps forward.

The figure whirled to face him, and as it turned in surprise, an egg slipped to the barn's wood floor and shattered.

Gus gasped. Inside the egg had been a nearly fully formed duckling. He could see its orange beak and webbed feet, perfect miniatures of those of a grown duck. The head flopped to the side, its face distorted by bulbous yellow eyes, still closed, and the dark down was clumped and spiked with wetness, as if the duck had been drowning in its shell.

"Look what you did!" Gus's voice rose almost to a wail.

The figure did not look at him. Instead, its hands came up and covered its face.

"*Escuse*. I'm sorry," a small voice said between the fingers. "I didn't mean to drop the egg."

"Who are you?" Gus demanded as he took another step forward.

"Louise. I'm Louise Lavictoire."

She looked up at last. Her nose was red, and her cheeks were streaked where tears had cut a path through the dirt. "I am *très, très* sorry."

"What are you *doing* here?" Gus pressed. He was close to tears himself, standing there looking at the baby duck lying dead on the barn floor. It nearly made him sick to his stomach.

"I was in the store and I heard Madame Amsler talking about the ducks in her barn," she explained. "I just wanted to see one. I've never seen a baby duck before."

"They're not her ducks," Gus corrected her. "And you just killed one before it even hatched."

"I know," Louise said, sniffling. She wiped her nose on her arm and then put her hands together behind her. "I said I was sorry. If I could, I'd put it back in the shell and paste it together again. But I know you can't do that. And anyway, you scared me. If you hadn't snuck up on me like some spy, I wouldn't have jumped and dropped the egg. So maybe this is your fault."

Her quick change of attitude gave Gus pause. Already he could see signs that butting heads with this girl would be like banging his head against an oak tree. And maybe he did share some of the blame for startling her. In any event, somebody had to show a little remorse for the duckling's fate, and Louise Lavictoire looked as though she'd gotten over hers in an instant, so that left only him to grieve.

Louise's tears had dried, and Gus found himself looking into two dark eyes that were growing more defiant by the second.

Suddenly, he had a thought. He strode over to the shattered egg and knelt down to study the duckling.

"What are you doing?" Louise asked, her voice a little softer, suggesting perhaps that she was sorry for the duckling's death, after all.

"I thought maybe if I could figure out how far along the

ducklings are, then I'd know when they're going to hatch," Gus said. His grandmother called this making lemonade from lemons, and he figured this was as good a time as any to make lemonade.

Louise knelt, too. Up close, Gus could tell she was about his age. But he was clean, or relatively so, while she was filthy. Her short hair was clotted with grease and dirt. Grime coated her arms, turning her at least two shades darker than she ought to have been, and her hands were the dirtiest hands Gus had ever seen. Her fingernails were nearly black. The only clean part of her seemed to be where the tears had coursed down her cheeks.

Gus picked up a piece of hay and poked at the duckling's body. He could see two stubby wings, two bulging eye sockets, two tiny webbed feet, a pale orange bill. He didn't know anything about unhatched ducklings, but it looked to him that about everything that should be there was there. In fact, there was so *much* there that the duckling looked almost too big to have fit in the shell. Gus thought it had to have been as cramped and dark in that shell as it was under his bed the other day when he tried to retrieve his baseball.

After a minute of studying the duckling, Gus said, "I don't know why they haven't hatched. I can't see anything that's missing."

"Maybe they're just not ready to breathe yet," Louise volunteered. "My mama had a baby once that died. The doctor said he just wasn't strong enough to breathe."

Gus looked up. "You talk funny," he said. "Where're you from?"

"Canada," she said.

"Then what are you doing down here?" Gus asked. He wasn't sure exactly how far away the Canadian border was, but it was clear she hadn't driven to the Amsler farm, and he knew it was too far to walk.

"My papa has a farm. On Cherry Hill," she said, pointing down the road.

"Where's that?" Gus asked.

"You go down this road a ways, and then go left up Cherry Hill," she told him.

"How'd you get here?" he asked.

"I walked," she said.

"How far?"

"Two miles, maybe," she said.

"You're willing to walk four miles to see a duck egg?" Gus asked, quickly doubling those two miles in his head. He could hardly believe anyone would expend that much energy to see an egg.

"I didn't know all you had was eggs. I've seen plenty of eggs. I thought I would get to see a baby duck. I never saw a baby duck up close before," she said, as if walking four miles to see a duck instead of a duck egg made more sense.

"Well, I wish I had a duck to show you," Gus said, standing up. "For that matter, I wish I had a duck to show me."

He glanced around and spotted a spade leaning against the wall.

"Come on, we'll bury it," he said.

He scooped up the duckling with the shovel and walked outside. They both surveyed the landscape, and finally Gus pointed with his nose toward the slope going down to the pond. They found a quiet spot near the water's edge where cattails grew and some young willows had taken root. Gus laid the duckling down and dug a hole. Then he lowered the duckling into it and replaced the dirt.

He started to leave, but Louise hung back.

"I think we should name it, and maybe we should say something," she said. "I don't think it's right to just walk away."

"We can't name it," Gus protested. "It's a duck. Besides, we don't know whether it was a boy or a girl."

"Then how about 'Babe'?" Louise suggested.

"That's a girl's name," Gus said with disgust.

"What about Babe Ruth?" Louise said. "He's not a girl."

So they named the duckling Babe. Louise used a pebble to scratch the name on a stone they found lying nearby. Afterward, she lifted the stone to her chest and then laid it on top of the dirt with great ceremony.

"Now," Louise turned to Gus, "you need to say something."

"Like what?" Gus asked. He was unfamiliar with the rituals of death and funerals, and he couldn't think of anything appropriate to say at the grave of a dead duckling.

"Erpose en paix," Louise said after a pause.

"What does that mean?" Gus asked.

"How do you say it? I think it means 'rest in peace,'" Louise explained, waving her hands in the air as if helping to lift the duckling's soul toward heaven.

"How come you know French?" Gus asked. He was impressed that someone who was about his age could speak a foreign language. The only words he knew in another language were "Heil, Hitler!" and he only knew those because he'd heard them so often on the radio.

"It's what we spoke in Canada," Louise said. "Before we came here."

Back up on the road, Louise and Gus stopped.

"My mama will be wanting me," Louise said. She looked at her feet. "If I could fix the duck, I would, but dead is dead. I'm sorry."

"There are still five eggs left," Gus said. The duckling's death had been a mixed blessing. He was sorry to lose even one of the remaining eggs, but now he had proof that something was growing inside them. He had renewed hope. They had to hatch soon. The duckling that had died had clearly filled the egg. How much bigger could the other ducklings grow before they burst out into the world?

"I'd still like to see a baby duck, a live one," Louise said. "If you would let me."

"I guess so. . . . I'll call you when they start hatching," said Gus, who was secretly pleased to have an excuse to crank up the big wooden telephone on the kitchen wall.

"We don't have a telephone," Louise said. "I don't understand how you can send your voice through the air like that, like magic."

"I don't know how they work, either," Gus admitted. "But I'll find some way to let you know when the time comes."

That night for supper, Gus and his grandparents ate peas, mashed potatoes, and more potted meat. It was going to be a long war, Gus thought, if that was all they were going to eat until the men came home.

"Who was that I saw you with when I was getting up from my nap?" his grandfather asked as he passed Gus the mashed potatoes for the second time.

"Louise Lavictoire," Gus said. He drew out the unfamiliar name, trying to pronounce it the way Louise had. He decided not to mention for the moment that she had killed one of his ducklings, even if it had been an accident. Instead, he spooned out a goodly pile of mashed potatoes and slathered them with oleo.

"Lavictoire. René Lavictoire," Gus's grandfather said. "We know that name, don't we?"

"Aren't the Lavictoires the family from Quebec that settled on Cherry Hill three or four years ago?" Gus's grandmother asked.

"Where's Quebec?" Gus asked.

"Canada," his grandmother said.

"That's where she said they used to live," Gus said.

"Well, what in the world was that child doing all the way over here?" his grandmother asked. "She must live at least two miles from here."

"She wanted to see the ducks," Gus explained.

"She walked over to see the ducks?" his grandfather asked in surprise.

"Yep," Gus said. "Four miles to see a duck. And all she got to see were the eggs."

"Bless her heart," his grandmother said. "I wouldn't think she'd have the strength to walk that far for such a flimsy reason."

"Why not?" Gus asked. Four miles was a fair distance, but he thought he could walk that far, maybe farther, especially if he had a good mind to.

"Well, I hear that whole family is sickly," his grandmother said, helping herself to corn relish. "Everyone in Miller's Run knows they're poor as church mice. Too bad for them they're not Yankee Protestant church mice. No sirree. Those Quebecers are all pope-worshiping Catholics with more mouths to feed than they can fill. Gossip has it that those French-Canadians marry their cousins and uncles and half-sisters. It wouldn't surprise me if a goodly number of those children were born idiots. When I was a child, everyone knew that the Quebecer families who roamed all over the countryside were thieves and beggars."

"I remember that," his grandfather agreed. "Everyone knew you couldn't trust one as far as you could throw him. Now they just buy up a little piece of land and settle down as if they belonged. But they don't. And it's official. Wasn't more than ten years ago that the state of Vermont was telling them to go back where they came from. Said the Quebecers were just watering down the good, God-fearing Yankee stock. Now they're taking land from good families who could do something with it. Seems like just a different kind of thievery."

"What your grandpa says is true, Gus. There isn't a soul in town who wouldn't be happy to see them go. Did Louise seem—how should I say it—soft in the head?" Gus's grandmother asked.

"No! I liked her," Gus protested. True, she had killed one of his ducks, but it *was* partially his fault. He'd startled her; it had been an accident. He was ready to give her a second chance, especially since the prospect of finding other friends this summer didn't look promising. He wasn't quite as ready as his grandparents seemed to be to transport her over the border with her family and all their belongings, at least not just because she was French Canadian. She couldn't help that.

"She seems awfully nice for a thief," Gus added meekly. "And she speaks real good English."

"Well, it's a relief to hear that they're not all idiots," his grandmother said as she rose from the table and began clearing it. "And you could use a friend, and maybe she could, too. Being nice to the less fortunate never hurt anyone. But keep an eye on her. The first time you catch her stealing something will be the last time she'll be welcome here."

Gus stood up and gathered his dishes and carried them over to the sink.

"After you feed the pig and check the eggs, don't wander off too far, Gus," his grandfather reminded him. "It's Tuesday. Our night to spot."

Gus loved Tuesday nights. He ran awkwardly to the pigpen, trying not to spill the slops, and threw them over the fence without bothering to watch out for the nasty sow. After that, he checked on the eggs. They lay quietly under the light, just as they had every night since he had put them there. The

*X*s and *Y*s were fading, worn off by the regular baths he gave the eggs and his handling of them. He turned them and gently nudged them together so there was no gap where the broken egg had been. He hoped they wouldn't start hatching in the night. He was so afraid of missing it.

Then he went back into the house, turned on the radio, and lay down on the floor to listen to Fibber McGee and his antics until darkness fell, but he was asleep before the program even started. His grandfather woke him a little before ten, just as Fibber let loose with his last wisecrack, and they walked off the back porch and up the yard a bit until they came to his aunt's old playhouse. No one had played there for years. The gray paint was peeling, and the small green shutters, painted to match those on the farmhouse, had long since broken off. They lay in the grass beside the playhouse like fallen soldiers. But the house itself was sturdy and had benches lining the inside walls and windows or a door on every side.

Gus and his grandfather each took a seat and settled down to watch the night sky. It was one of the more exciting things Gus did on the farm, where the days and his solitary work in the garden and barn were busy but filled with a certain monotony now that the cows weren't around to liven things up. His grandfather was a spotter for the Civil Air Patrol. His job once a week was to watch the night sky for either of Germany's zeppelins or any other German planes or airships. Fortunately, the United States believed that only Germany's enormous dirigibles were capable of making a trans-Atlantic flight and attacking cities along the

East Coast. So even though the probability of an attack was small, the United States couldn't let its guard down and ignore the possibility that war might break out on its own soil.

At first, Gus couldn't imagine why any German bombers would be interested in Vermont—it was nothing but farms, as far he could see—but his grandfather had explained that factories in southern Vermont were manufacturing equipment that was needed to make tanks and planes. If the German bombers could destroy the factories, it would cripple the country's ability to produce machines for the war. Plus, Vermont was on the way to bigger places if the German planes came in north over the Pole, heading somewhere like New York City or Washington or even Boston.

Outside, under the stars on Tuesday nights, Gus felt as if he were doing something to help the United States win the war. The Civil Air Patrol had to identify every type of aircraft that went overhead, and then alert officials if it was anything suspicious. Even though Gus and his grandfather were really only keeping an eye out for zeppelins, they had spotter cards that helped them distinguish Stukas from Messerschmitts and dozens of other types of enemy aircraft. Gus studied the cards during the day, but at night they weren't very helpful. All you could see in the sky were lights. The newspapers ran articles trying to train people not to look directly at moving lights in the night sky but to fix their eyes slightly off center and watch from the edge of their field of vision. At first, Gus had thought this was stupid, but once he'd tried it a few times, he concluded the newspaper writers were right. You could actually see a lot more at night by not looking directly at the thing you wanted to see.

Even so, Gus's grandfather wasn't taking any chances; he was also teaching him to identify different types of planes by sound.

Together, they sat for a couple of hours without hearing anything except the whirring of cicadas and the occasional piping squeak of a bat winging nearby on its nightly quest for insects. Looking out the windows, they could see that the night sky was clear and spangled with stars. If any plane did appear, they would have no trouble listening to the thrum of its engines as it moved across the great black dome.

For a long time, the only light was the glow of Gus's grandfather's pipe. The pungent perfume of tobacco filled the little house, and the glow in the pipe bowl alternately flared and died as his grandfather breathed in and out.

"When the eggs hatch, what will happen?" Gus asked.

"*If* they hatch, Gus. *If* they hatch," his grandfather made a point of saying, "then we'll need to build a brooder. That's a big box with a warming light hanging over it. You'll need hay and water and duck feed. I've been putting off fussing with all that until it looked like the eggs might actually hatch."

"I think they're going to," Gus told him.

"What makes you say that?" his grandfather asked. In the starry silence, Gus could hear the rasping sound of his grandfather rubbing his hand up and down his whiskers. It was something he did whenever he was quietly pondering a situation. "They might all be dead and you're just taking care of a clutch of duds that are never going to hatch."

"I dropped one today," Gus said, afraid to bring any more criticism down on the heads of the poor Lavictoires. "It had a baby duck in it. It almost looked alive."

"Did it?" His grandfather laughed softly. "Well, then, maybe we should get busy and get ready for them. When they come, you're going to find out just how demanding babies can be."

"Can we start tomorrow?" Gus asked.

"No reason not to," his grandfather answered. "Once they're here, they're going to need everything at once."

Then they saw it, a pinpoint of light rising up above the rim of the bowl and starting to trace a path across the night sky. Seconds later they heard it, a soft drone like the buzz of a mosquito flying around their ears at night as they lay in bed. Together, they sat quietly, listening, tracking the sound as it moved steadily overhead.

"It's okay. It's one of ours," Gus's grandfather said finally.

Gus didn't realize that he had been holding his breath until his grandfather spoke. Every plane made him think of his father, so far away and learning to fly, going up in contraptions that humans built to defy God's natural laws. Or at least that's what his grandmother said. Gus didn't think of it that way, though. As much as he missed his father, he also envied him, wishing for himself the excitement of barreling down a runway and lifting off into the silken air and the sky.

"I never hear an airplane without thinking of your father," his grandfather said, as if reading his thoughts.

"When you do think he'll be home?" Gus asked.

"I don't know. Nothing in life is fixed. Not even the stars in the sky. But if something has a home, it will usually return there when it can. That's true of bees and foxes and people. It's even true of ducks. It's possible the duck I killed was raised on our pond a year or two ago. We've almost always had ducks on the pond."

"But what about Dad? When will *he* come home?" Gus asked.

"That's hard to say. He's got you and your mother to come home to," his grandfather said. By now the plane had traversed the inky sky and disappeared over the opposite horizon, but they could still hear its pulsating engine in the night stillness. "He'll be home as soon as he can, as soon as we win this war."

Chapter Three

Two days later, Gus was in the barn admiring the brooder he had built with his grandfather. They had constructed it out of boards salvaged from a pile of lumber long abandoned in the barn loft. The brooder looked like the sandbox he had played in as a toddler in the park, but with higher sides. To keep the ducklings warm once they hatched, Gus and his grandfather planned to take the light bulb from the incubator and suspend it about a foot above the brooder. Otherwise, everything was ready. Gus's grandfather had sent him all over the barn hunting for an old chicken waterer. Finally, Gus had been lucky to find it, buried in hay and covered with dirt, but with its glass jar unbroken. As long as the war was going on, even ordinary things like glass were scarce. Gus scrubbed the waterer until it shone, and he filled the jar with fresh water and screwed on the top, which was really an upside-down tray. Then he inverted the whole thing, and air bubbled up into the jar and water filled the tray. A twenty-pound bag of poultry meal was propped against the near wall. He'd buy two bags of meal, his grandfather said;

after that, the ducks would have to learn to scavenge for insects and grass.

At first, Gus didn't pay any attention to the sound coming from the incubator. He was sitting beside it on his upturned milk pail, a book balanced on his knees, writing a letter to his mother. He had very little news to share about himself. The garden was growing as crazily as Jack's beanstalk, and the eggs—well, they were still just eggs. He imagined his mother lying as placidly as an egg in her chaise hour after hour, and it made him want to write something that would make her laugh.

> *Dear Mom,*
> *Knock, knock.*
> *Who's there?*
> *Dodo.*
> *Dodo who?*
> *Dodo what to say.*
> *Ha, ha! Dad wrote and said that all rookie pilots are called dodos, because they're big and heavy and can't fly. I guess that makes you and me dodos, too. He also says he has room inspection every morning. So do I. Where did Grandma learn how to be a drill sergeant?*

Gus turned the piece of paper sideways and started to write across what he'd already written, something his grandmother had taught him so he could squeeze as much news as possible onto a single sheet.

Grandpa and I built a brooder for the ducklings for when they hatch, which I hope will be soon. Then I'll have news. I hope you are feeling better. I miss you.

Love,
Your son, Gus

Gus was rereading his note when he finally paid attention to the sound. It was so faint and small that he assumed it was coming from the nest of one of the phoebes that favored the intersecting rafters high overhead. From waiting patiently below and observing them, Gus could tell that most of the phoebe eggs had hatched. Now the phoebes passed their days busily flying in and out of the barn, their mouths no doubt filled with squished mosquitos and beetles for their demanding broods. But the chirping didn't stop, as it often did when even insatiable baby birds finally settled down to sleep.

Gus perked up. Hardly daring to trust his hearing, he leaned over the incubator. The sound was coming from the eggs, faint chirps that struck his ears with a desperate urgency. His heart racing, he leaned farther over and looked closely at the eggs, and now he could see cracks that hadn't been there yesterday. In two eggs, he could see tiny holes, not much bigger than pinheads, and beaks pushing in and out, working away like tiny hammers to chip away at the fragile shells.

"They're hatching!" Gus shouted. He raced to the doorway and shouted again. "They're hatching!"

His grandmother arrived first, panting and fanning herself with her apron. His grandfather was second, limping into the barn as fast as his tired knees would allow.

All three of them leaned over the incubator and stared.

"Heaven's mercy," his grandmother said. "Who would have thought! Hope *does* have feathers."

His grandfather just chuckled. "You're in for it now, Gus."

They stood around for perhaps fifteen minutes, waiting for the first miracle, but the ducklings were taking their time. Eventually, Gus's grandmother said she had to get back to the kitchen. She was stewing rhubarb, and it needed attention or it would burn the bottom of the pot.

Gus's grandfather started to leave, too. "I can't stand like I used to, Gus. You'll just have to be patient. This could take all afternoon, maybe longer. That shell is so thin you could crush it with your fingers just by snapping them, but to those ducklings that shell is as solid as a wall. Just don't help them," he warned sternly. "If a duckling's not strong enough to break out of the egg on its own, it won't survive anyway."

As his grandfather approached the door, Gus had an inspiration. "Can I go get Louise?" he asked.

"How will you get there and back in time?" his grandfather asked. "If you walk the whole four miles, you might just miss the great spectacle yourself."

"I'll take that bike." Gus pointed to a shadowy corner of the barn where he'd found an old bike while rummaging around for the chicken waterer. The long-forgotten bike was leaning against one of the stalls. There was little grace in the design, but it had everything it needed. Enormous fenders, most of the red paint long since chipped away, bloomed over the spoked wheels, and the handlebars stuck out like praying mantis elbows. The bike was dusty and covered with rust, but it still had its tires, though they needed some air.

"Well, I'll be," his grandfather said. He took off his hat and scratched his head. "That was your father's bicycle. I had no idea it was still around. And if I had, I'd probably have turned it in during the last scrap drive."

"Can I take it?" Gus asked.

"Does it have brakes? Can you ride it?" his grandfather asked.

"Yep," Gus assured him. He had scooted around the barn on it the day before. "But the tires are flat. Can you put air in them?"

"I think I can handle that," his grandfather said. He limped over to his workshelves and rummaged around under them until he found the tire pump. "Bring it over here."

Gus wheeled the bike over, and his grandfather unscrewed the nozzle caps on both tires. While Gus held the bike, his grandfather pushed down on the pump handle. They both watched the tires grow firm and taut.

"I don't know whether they'll hold, but that's the best I can do," his grandfather declared. "Do you know how to get to the Lavictoires'?"

"Not really," Gus said, aware that precious time was passing.

His grandfather pointed down the hill. "Go straight for about one mile. You'll see the turn for Cherry Hill. Go left, up that hill for about another mile. When you come to the sorriest farm in all of Miller's Run, you're there," he said.

Gus took off, pedaling furiously. The first part was easy, all downhill from his grandparents' farm. When he saw the turn for Cherry Hill, he started uphill. After ten minutes, he wondered if there was any top to this spine-rattling road of rocks. His face burned, and he could feel his shirt clinging to his sweaty back.

Then he saw it—the sorriest farm in all of Miller's Run, maybe in all of creation. Looking around, he tried to imagine the accumulation of stuff inside his grandfather's barn, multiplied tenfold and turned inside out. The yard, such as it was, was strewn with wreckage: broken mowers, washing machines, and unidentifiable pieces of farm machinery; splintered wooden tubs that had once served who-knows-what purposes; a tipped-over sewing machine treadle; barbed wire; a truck sunk to its axles in dried mud, with grass grown up around it as if it had taken root. The house itself was much like his grandparents' house—an old farm-house one-story high, with slanted windows in the gables—but the roof on this one sagged, and it could not have been wearing more than one gallon of paint spread across its cracked and warped clapboards. Fields surrounded the house on three sides, separated from the house and vegetable garden by rail wood fences that were falling down. In one place, a bony cow had stepped over the fallen fence and found some shade under an old apple tree. It was contentedly munching grass next to an old wagon that listed on broken axles like a ship gone aground. Laundry flapped on a line out back, but the clothes and sheets looked gray and dingy. Everywhere, the place looked unkempt and uncared for. Even the vegetable garden looked untidy, overrun with weeds and vines strangling the young plants. In the middle of it stood a scarecrow wearing a faded blue-flowered dress, but the crosstie was broken and the arms hung down, as if the scarecrow itself had given up.

Gus could hear the shrieks of young children coming from inside the house. Mustering his courage, he leaned his bicycle against the truck marooned in the front yard and knocked on the door. No one answered. He knocked again, louder. This time someone yanked the door open so hard that Gus stumbled backward. The sound of shrieking increased, but it was not frightened shrieking; it was more the sound Gus could remember making himself when he was little and in high spirits.

"Eh?" asked a dirty little child of about seven or eight, boy or girl he could not tell. Like Louise the day she visited the barn, this child wore patched coveralls and a torn plaid shirt.

"I want to talk to Louise," Gus explained.

The door slammed in his face, and he stood there feeling stupid, unsure if the child had even understood him. He shifted from one foot to the other, trying to decide whether to go or stay. The ducks might be hatching at this very moment.

Suddenly, the door opened again. Louise stood in the doorway. She grinned when she saw him.

"Hi," she said, as if she'd been expecting him.

"The—the eggs are hatching," he stammered. "You said you wanted to come and see. I brought a bike. Maybe we could both ride it back." He turned and pointed toward the bike, afraid she would not be able to find it amid the other items littering the yard.

"I have to finish my work. I'm washing faces," she said and opened the door wider. "It will take a couple more minutes."

Gus assumed the opened door was an invitation and followed Louise into the house. What he saw stunned him. The front parlor looked as if a tornado had gone through it. Stuffing overflowed from the couch. A cracked mirror hung on the wall beside a rusty potbellied stove. The carpet was threadbare, its design long worn away by passing feet.

The kitchen, where a large tub of water sat in the middle of the floor, was in shambles. Drawers hung open, dripping their contents of tablecloths and towels. Unwashed pots lay abandoned on the long plank table, and one child, perhaps the one who had answered Gus's knock, had buried his arm in one of the pots and was greedily eating whatever he could scrape up. The windows were cloudy with grime, and every curtain hung limply from nails in the frames, as if they were exhausted by the responsibility of spreading cheer in such surroundings. Above all this, a single light bulb dangled from a black cord. It looked out of place, as if electricity had come to Miller's Run not five years ago but only yesterday and the Lavictoires didn't know what to do with it.

In the middle of this disarray, Louise spoke sharply. *"Fermez la!"* she said. "Quiet!"

To Gus's surprise, the children immediately quieted down.

Now that the mayhem had subsided and he could think,

he counted the children. They all looked small for their age, as Louise did, but their faces were a truer measure. Two boys were probably around ten. Two more, the ones playing in the water by dipping their hands in it and flicking it at each other, were probably a bit too young for school. The smallest one, who was running around without a stitch of clothing, was just a toddler. All of them were scrawny; Gus thought they looked like his grandmother's chickens when they got wet. But as near as he could tell, none of them looked like an idiot, as his grandmother had said.

"*Faut y'aller astheure,*" Louise said. "*Coup d'a coup! Les bébés sont nés.*"

Their faces lit up, and they looked at Gus hopefully. Clearly, she had told them about the duck eggs and her trip to Gus's barn.

"*Wheezie, on peut venir aussi?*" one of them pleaded. The two medium-sized Lavictoires grabbed their older sister's arm and tried to pull her toward the door, looking themselves like baby birds eager for lunch. Without understanding a single word of what Louise had said, Gus could see that everyone wanted to come see the ducks hatch. His heart sank a little.

"*Non. Il faut aller maintenant,*" Louise said, stamping her foot on the floor to show that she meant *right now*.

She shook her hand loose and started drying off as many faces as she could reach. Noses and eyes emerged from the grime bright and shiny, as if Louise had been polishing pots, not cheeks.

The clothes the little one put on were clean but dingy, shabbier than those Gus took off at the end of the day. When everyone was dressed, they headed toward the back door, although two of them turned to look at Louise with the kind of eyes that will usually get a dog an extra treat.

"Henri, André!" Louise called after them. The two older boys stopped. She pointed toward the tub.

They came back and grabbed its handles. Staggering out, they pretended to be musclemen, each with one twig-thin arm on a tub handle and one arched over his head. Gus had to laugh.

"Let me tell Mama," Louise said as she also headed out the back door.

He could see her with her mother and a big laundry tub, and he could almost eavesdrop on them, but they were chattering in words he didn't understand. Now that quiet had descended on the house, he could hear a radio going somewhere. Louise returned in a minute. She raced toward the front door, pausing briefly to turn off the radio in the parlor. Gus followed and didn't say anything, but he was puzzled.

"It's my English lesson," Louise explained breezily. "Every day I listen so I can get better and better. I start with *The Farmer's Special with Uncle Jim* in the morning and end with Jack Benny, but my favorite show is *Ma Perkins,* and I try not to miss *The World Today,* so I can tell Papa what the news is, but sometimes we're eating supper then, and sometimes he's already asleep."

"I wondered why you spoke English so good and no one else in your family can," Gus admitted.

"Papa says he's too old, Mama says she's too tired,"

Louise said. "You tell me if I say something stupid. I want to get it right."

"Well, right now, we'd better get going or we'll miss the whole thing," Gus said.

For the first time, it occurred to him that the bike had only one small seat. Louise looked at it for a few seconds and told Gus to hold the bike steady while she climbed up and sat across the handlebars. Then they set off down the dirt road. Gus could hardly see over Louise's shoulder, and Louise was less than vigilant about pointing out potholes and rocks in the road. Once they spilled, and Louise flew off the handlebars and landed on her backside in the road with an *Oomph!* Gus fell with the bike tangled up in his legs, but neither was hurt. Laughing, they climbed back on and rode as far as they could. Gus's legs finally gave out as they were climbing the last stretch toward his grandparents' farm. Louise slid off as the bike ground to a halt in the dust, and they ran the last several hundred yards, Gus pushing the bicycle and fearful that the ducklings had hatched and the show was over.

But it wasn't. Two more eggs had holes in them. Most of the cracks were wider, and the noises coming from the eggs were louder and more urgent. Louise and Gus sat watching through all the rest of the long, hot afternoon. Gus's grandmother brought them sassafrass water at one point. When she entered the barn, Louise immediately stood up.

"Grandma, this is Louise," Gus said, tearing his eyes away from the eggs long enough to introduce them.

"Pleased to meet you," Louise said, and she stuck out her hand.

Gus's grandmother considered her blackened fingernails and dirty arm, and then pointed with her nose to the glasses she was holding to indicate that she had no free hand to offer in return. Louise blushed and snatched her hand back.

"Nice to meet you, too, Louise," Gus's grandmother said as she offered them both cold glasses glistening with condensation.

"Thank you, ma'am," Louise said, and Gus saw his grandmother's face soften. She took up a position next to the brooder and looked at the eggs expectantly.

"Gettin' born can take a while," Louise observed.

"I'll bet your mother has learned that through long experience," Gus's grandmother said, but her tone was kind.

Gus's grandfather came out after his nap, his hair still tousled from sleep and standing upright in spikes. He was there when the first duckling emerged. It was wet and dark, just like the one that had died on the barn floor, but this one staggered around a few steps, as if it were drunk. Its eyes were tiny black beads as glossy as beetles. Eventually, it settled down on its little orange feet, closed its eyes, and sat very still, apparently exhausted by the day's events.

Gus and Louise could not take their eyes off it.

"Put it under the light for now, to dry it off and keep it warm," Gus's grandfather said. "But when they've all hatched, move the light over to the brooder, the way I showed you, and move the ducklings over there."

By suppertime, all but two of the eggs had hatched. The first duckling to hatch had dried out and fluffed up. Too young for feathers, it was covered in a soft yellow down that darkened to brown at the top of its head and along its pathetic little wings. The other two ducklings, resting as they dried themselves under the incubator light, were starting to look like ducks, not small drowned birds. All three ducklings were chirping and peeping, and obviously interested in something to eat.

Gus's grandmother came out again around six o'clock.

"Aren't they adorable?" she said, unable to resist nudging one with her finger. It peeped nervously and scrambled toward the comfort of the light. "Louise, I think Mr. Amsler had better take you home in the truck. It's suppertime, and your mother must be getting worried about you."

Louise looked at Gus.

"It's okay. You've seen most of it," Gus said. "There are only two left. I'll tell you about them. You can come back tomorrow."

Before she left, Louise helped Gus move the light to the brooder.

Then they went back to the incubator and moved the three soft, squirming ducklings one at a time. They cupped the baby ducks in their hands close to their chests and were amazed at their lightness. Gus's duckling felt as if it were made of nothing but air as warm and soft as breath. But he could feel the gentle pulsing of the duck's breast as its tiny heart beat a steady staccato against his hands. Gus and Louise looked at each other. Gus smiled shyly and blushed. Without knowing why, he felt embarrassed, as if he had been caught by his friends telling his mother he loved her.

Once in the brooder, the ducklings sought out the water and plunged their bills eagerly into the tin cup. As they drank, big bubbles gurgled up inside the water jar. Then they found the meal and picked at it, not eating any, as near as Gus could tell, but just pushing it around, trying it out. Finally, they settled down under the light and closed their eyes, content with their day's work.

Louise left in the truck, which rattled down the dirt road, leaving a billowing cloud of dust in its wake. Gus moved the last two eggs to the brooder and put them in the light bulb's glow, where they would be warm and safe.

After supper, on his way back from feeding the pig, he looked in on the ducklings. One was stirring. It struggled to its feet and tottered to the water and then to the meal, before collapsing and closing its eyes in the same second. The two others slept on. The two unhatched eggs lay quietly in the hay. One had a few cracks, but Gus couldn't see any holes.

Just before bedtime, he and his grandfather took a flashlight and went out to the barn for one last check. The three ducklings were piled together so closely that Gus couldn't tell where one began and another ended. They were sleeping soundly in the warm glow of the light. Gus moved the two eggs closer to the light's warmth.

"Enjoy them tonight," his grandfather told him. "Things will be pretty busy from here on out."

"It's a miracle they hatched," Gus said. He hadn't known until that afternoon how great his fear had been that the eggs would never hatch.

"New life is always a miracle," Gus's grandfather said. "In all the years I farmed, I never went out in the morning and found a new calf without thinking it was one of God's blessings. And that may be true," he added, turning to look at Gus, "but it's you and not God who has to take care of these ducklings. You brought them into this world, and you're the one responsible for them."

Chapter Four

Gus was up at daybreak. He dressed in a flash. Dressing went faster now that he almost never bothered with shoes. Who needed them anyway, when everyone was trying to save leather and rubber for the fighting men? He flew through the kitchen, where he noticed that his grandmother was sliding a pan of eggs poached in milk into the oven. Without even favoring her with a hello, he sprinted for the barn.

Early as it was, his grandfather was already there, standing in the doorway. He was leaning on the door frame and chewing on his pipe stem. The pipe wasn't lit. Gus knew his grandfather never smoked in the barn because of all the dry hay.

"Good morning, young man," he said, taking the pipe from his mouth. "Are you ready?"

"Ready for what?" Gus asked, suddenly afraid that something terrible had happened in the night.

"To be a mother," his grandfather said.

"What do you mean?" Gus asked, even more confused.

"Ducks imprint on the first animal they see," his grandfather explained. "That means they think whatever they see first is their mother. Usually, of course, it *is* their mother."

"Have you gone in to look at them?" Gus asked.

"Heavens, no!" Gus's grandfather said. "I don't want a bunch of fool ducks following me around all summer thinking I'm their mother. I'm waiting for *you* to go in first. Be my guest." He laughed, and made a sweeping gesture with his hat. Then he headed toward the house.

Gus crept into the barn as if he were a GI scouting an enemy position. His grandfather's words flashed in his head like a blinking red light, and he decided to move slowly until he had a better sense of what this imprinting business was all about.

One of the remaining eggs had hatched in the night. The shell lay splintered beneath the light, its inside surface a web of fine red lines and dried specks of yolk. All four ducklings were waddling around, dabbling in the water tray and pecking at the meal. None of them was more than four inches tall, and all were covered in the same soft yellow down, as insubstantial as milkweed fluff. Gus could tell which duckling had hatched last. One of its webbed feet was deformed, and it stumbled more than usual when it walked.

As soon as the ducklings saw Gus, they set up a racket that sounded like the Hallelujah Chorus at Christmas in his church back home. They danced nervously under the warm light, and kept their tiny black eyes glued on every move he made.

Gus grabbed the milk pail and sat down to watch. He had no idea what the ducklings wanted him to do or what their mother would have done had she lived. The ducklings were pretty small and fragile, after all, but they seemed to have great expectations of Gus. Finally, they just sat and looked at each other. Ten minutes later his grandfather returned to the barn to fetch him.

"Your grandmother says your breakfast will be so cold or so hard cooked, it'll be fit only for the pig if you don't come in now and eat it," he said. But he didn't seem to be in any hurry himself.

"What about the last egg, Grandpa? Will it hatch?"

"If it hasn't by now, it's probably not going to," his grandfather said. "Usually, the mother lays her eggs all at once, and they pretty much hatch all at once. I'd say it's a dud. But you did pretty well, I guess. Four out of five."

"What should I do with it?" Gus asked.

"Feed it to the pig," his grandfather said. "You can leave it until tonight, and then add it to the slops. It's best not to let it lie around. If it's rotten and it breaks open, the air in the barn won't be worth breathing. You also might think about killing that little one, the one with the crooked foot."

Gus was horrified. "Why?"

"Because most damaged animals don't make it," his grandfather said. "It's nature's way of keeping the stock strong."

"Do I have to?" asked Gus, who couldn't even bear the idea of killing a duckling he'd worked so hard to hatch.

"No," his grandfather said. "I'm just saying you should think about it. It'll probably die sooner or later anyway. That's the way these things usually go."

"What do I have to do now?" Gus asked with relief. "I mean, to take care of them."

"Keep them warm. Keep the hay dry so they don't rot their feet. And make sure they have food and water," his grandfather said. "Don't handle them too much. They're not kittens. The rest is up to nature."

That morning, working in the garden was agony. Gus wanted to be up and doing, caring for the ducklings and watching them, as if they would grow before his eyes. But his grandmother had him picking potato bugs off the potato plants and dropping them into a tin can, at the bottom of which were two inches of kerosene. When he filled the can with bugs, she said she'd give him a penny. Gus plucked at the small striped beetles and dropped them into the kerosene. There, they squirmed briefly and then, Gus guessed, died a gruesome death by drowning. The work hurt his legs because he had to crouch, so eventually he decided just to crawl along the dusty row, pushing the can in front of him. It was easier on his knees but harder on his overalls. He hoped his grandmother had some patches ready for later in the summer.

He was standing in the barn admiring the ducklings after a dinner of dumplings and pan gravy when Louise appeared at his side.

"Hi," he said, surprised.

"What's the matter with that one?" she asked, pointing to the unhatched egg.

"Grandpa says it's a dud. I'm supposed to feed it to the pig tonight."

"Is that the one that hatched last night?" Louise asked. She squatted to get a closer look.

"Yes," Gus said. "There's something wrong with its foot, but it's still getting around okay."

They watched it stumble over to the meal and peck at it, then settle down right at the edge of the food dish and close its eyes. Together, they watched for another half hour, but that was the extent of the activity. Finally, Gus gave the ducklings fresh water and a half cup of fresh meal. They struck up another chorus at this intrusion and watched him closely, but they quickly settled down again.

"What are they doing?" Louise asked, laughing.

"Grandpa says they're imprinting. Since they don't have a real mother, they think I'm their mother," Gus explained.

"You?" Louise laughed again. Gus liked her laugh, but he was hurt by the unavoidable conclusion that she thought this development ridiculous.

"Who else do they have?" Gus asked. "I don't really know what imprinting means yet, but my grandpa said something about following me around. We'll see."

Together, Gus and Louise sorted through hay in the mow until they had put aside a pile of the freshest bedding they could find. When they finished, Louise said, "I have to go now. Mama wants me to do chores."

"I'll take you on the bike," Gus volunteered.

"That's fine," his grandfather said when Gus asked him. "But don't dawdle. There's something I want to teach you."

This time, Gus was prepared for the shock of Louise's house. He dropped her at the front door, amid ancient relics of rusted machinery and rotten potatoes gone to seed. Inside, he could hear a child crying and a woman yelling words he didn't recognize. The foreign sounds rang in his ears and stayed with him all the trip home.

As Gus wheeled his bike into the barn, he found his grandfather standing in front of his workshop shelves. The workshelf was piled with pliers and wrenches, wire cutters and cracked saucers filled with all the odd lots of nuts and screws that kept a farm and its machinery up and running. He had a rifle broken down. The stock, its wood the rich, dark color of chestnuts, glistened with the rubbing and polishing of many hands. The barrel was burnished and shiny with a fine coat of oil.

"What are you doing, Grandpa?" Gus asked.

"I'm going to give you a shooting lesson," his grandfather said without looking up. He brought the rifle to his shoulder and sighted down the barrel toward the wall.

"Really?" Gus's heart began to beat so fast he thought his grandfather could probably hear it. He had passed his grandfather's gun rack in the mudroom his whole life, but he had been told ever since he was three feet tall never to touch it.

"Grab some feed sacks and stuff them with hay, over there in the old horse stalls," his grandfather instructed him.

Gus rummaged around in a corner of the barn where a big pile of used feed bags had accumulated until he found two that were pretty dirty, though it was still easy to read "Burket Feed and Grain" on them. He saved the cleanest ones for his grandmother because he knew she bleached them until the writing had faded and then made them into tea towels or sewed them into tablecloths. He scrounged on the floor and in the old mangers, stuffing handful after handful of hay into the bags until they bulged like St. Nick's coat.

"Now carry them out behind the barn, well away from the pig. We don't want any accidents," his grandfather said.

This was more work than Gus expected. The sacks were heavier than he thought they would be, and carrying them meant having the prickly hay poke him in his face, tickle his nose, escape down his shirt, and almost suffocate him with its sharp, ripe odor. Eventually, he hauled the two sacks up into the field behind the barn and dropped them side by side.

His grandfather appeared carrying the rifle and an old newspaper with a black circle the size of a dinner plate drawn on it.

"Pin this up there against the sacks," he told Gus, handing him the newspaper and one of his grandmother's sewing pins. "And if you prick your finger, let's hope that's the only blood shed today."

Finally, with the target in place, he began the lesson. "I want you to remember two things," he said. "Never point a gun at anything you don't intend to shoot, including a man— although God forbid you should ever have to do such a thing. And when you walk with a rifle, even in the woods, always point it toward the ground."

Gus was so eager to get his hands on the gun that he barely heard his grandfather's instructions.

After what seemed like forever, his grandfather finally gave him the rifle. "This is a Winchester .30-30 lever-action deer rifle," he explained as he handed Gus the gun. "If you know what you're doing, you can drop a deer with it at a hundred yards. A man, too."

The rifle had a certain grace and balance. When Gus settled the stock against his shoulder and raised the gun with trembling hands to look along its sights, it fell into position so comfortably and naturally he thought of a bird coming home to roost. But the gun was unexpectedly heavy, too, and he wondered if he would ever be able to hold it steady enough to be a good shot.

His grandfather showed him how to aim by aligning the front and rear sights and how to load the magazine with cartridges. Gus liked the crisp ring of metal as he snapped the lever forward and then back to chamber a cartridge.

"Now aim for the feed sack and squeeze the trigger," his grandfather said.

Gus tried to do just what he'd been told. He looked down the long barrel until the circle on the newspaper seemed aligned with the sights. He tried to steady his hands. Finally, he wrapped his finger around the slender trigger and pulled. The gun exploded in his ears and kicked painfully against his shoulder. The concussion drove him a step backward and almost sat him on his backside. Everything went dark, and he realized with shame that his eyes were closed.

"Well, it's a good thing we aren't anywhere near the pig," his grandfather said, taking his hat off and using it to protect his eyes from the sun. He peered into the distance.

"Was I close?" Gus asked hopefully.

"I think that bullet's in the next county by now," his grandfather said. "Try again."

Gus chambered and shot, chambered and shot, and gradually he reached the point where he could hit one of the feed sacks every third shot or so, even though he never did hit the target. The sweat was pouring off his forehead and stinging his eyes. The rifle barrel, cool and firm an hour ago, was warm and slippery now. Gus's arms trembled with fatigue, and his shoulder throbbed. He imagined it probably had a bruise on it the size of a softball. He had a roaring in his ears and what felt like a permanent dent in his right cheek where it had rested on the stock. His grandfather, always a patient man, kept taking off his hat and wiping his forearm across his forehead.

"You haven't reached the point where you can shoot the baking powder out of a biscuit, but I think you're finally a greater danger to someone else than you are to yourself. Let's call it a day," his grandfather said.

"Do we have to?" Gus begged, but his heart wasn't in it.

As they walked back toward the barn, his grandfather said, "You can practice on any of the rifles or shotguns from now on without me. Just make sure the gun's empty when you're through, and that you clean it like you've seen me do a hundred times and put it away. And for Pete's sake, be careful. Don't go doing something foolish, like shooting off your foot."

"Why'd you teach me, Grandpa?" Gus asked.

"Every man ought to know how to shoot a gun," his grandfather answered. "Especially during a war, you never know who might show up on your doorstep, but now you know how to protect yourself if, God forbid, you ever have to."

"You mean I might have to shoot somebody?" Gus asked, aghast. Until then, he had had visions of perhaps going after a squirrel or a blackbird with one of his grandfather's smaller rifles, maybe the .22, although the thought of killing anything was new and took some getting used to.

"It's wartime," his grandfather repeated. "You never know."

In the evening, after supper, Gus carried the bucket of slops out to the pig. He stopped in the barn first and looked at the unhatched egg, hoping to see some evidence of life, some reason for hope. The four ducklings were waddling around the brooder gabbling and making regular deposits in the straw, but when Gus appeared, they rushed for the safety of the light and huddled there together like nervous old ladies, eyeing him warily. Only the egg was immobile. Reluctantly, Gus reached in and plucked it from its nest of straw. It was warm and almost smooth in his hand. It felt no different from the way the other eggs had felt. They had eventually burst open with life, but this one was a dud, just as his grandfather had said. He dropped it gently into the slop bucket, where it floated in the mush of old gravy, potato peelings, wilted dandelion greens, and water-logged bread, and carried everything out to the pig.

She was waiting for him. She left her piglets squealing in the mud over their abandonment and approached the fence looking as ungrateful as ever for Gus's faithful service. Gus heaved the bucket of slops over the top rail and turned and ran. If the egg split open when it hit the ground and revealed a fully formed duckling, he didn't want to see it. If the pig devoured the egg eagerly, he didn't want to see that, either. If the egg stank to high heaven, he didn't want to smell it. As his grandmother had said, it was a pity, and he didn't want any part of it.

Chapter Five

Over the next several days, Gus rushed out to tend to the ducklings even before he ate breakfast. Every morning, he removed all the dirty hay and replaced it with fresh. He poured out yesterday's water, which the ducklings had spoiled with meal, and filled the jar with clear, cold water. He saved what he could of the old meal, trying to make it last as long as he could, and replenished it from the dwindling supply.

At first, the ducklings greeted him with noisy alarm, but he made a point of being quiet and deliberate around them. "Hey, ducks," he called softly every time he put fresh water or meal in the brooder. "Hey, ducks."

By the third day, the ducklings stopped greeting his approach with terror. Instead, they scurried to a corner and waited, vigilant and gabbling in low tones among themselves, for him to perform his duties. By the fourth day, when he said "Hey, ducks," one of the ducklings came over and nipped him on the finger. He yanked his hand away, startled but unhurt, and then slowly lowered his hand back into the brooder. The duckling took another stab at him, and then, satisfied that Gus's finger wasn't some new kind of food, it turned its attention to the duck meal. The others quickly waddled over and joined the feast.

Gus was glad the ducklings were occupied for a little while. His grandfather had been to town already that morning and had returned with two letters for him, one from his mother and one from his father. Gus had stuffed them in the pocket of his overalls, and now he stepped on the ladder, swung himself up into the mow, and settled down in the hay to read. His mother's note barely filled the front of the sheet of paper.

> *Dear Gus,*
>
> *The weather has been lovely here and I have been able to spend many hours lying in the sunshine soaking up the clean Adirondack air. At night, I sleep on a long porch lined with beds, each filled with someone who, like me, is trying to get well so we can go home again. I imagine all the fresh air you're getting yourself, plus your grandmother's cooking, has put some inches and muscle on you. I hope the ducklings have hatched. Write me all about them in your next post card. I miss you.*
>
> *Much love,*
> *Mother*

Gus knew immediately how he was going to start his next letter to his mother:

> *Knock, knock.*
> *Who's there?*
> *Quack.*

Quack who?
I have four quacked egg shells and four ducklings.

And then he would tell her about them. He might even ask her what she recommended he do since the ducklings thought he was their mother. She had experience in that area that he lacked. He was only a thirteen-year-old city boy who knew nothing about mothering or ducks.

His father's letter was a little longer, but then again, Gus knew his life was a lot more exciting than his mother's, whose description of herself lying in a chaise on the lawn reminded him of a turtle basking in the sun on a log.

Hey, Buster,

You must be getting pretty big for your britches these days on Grandma's meals and farm chores. A farm is no place for the weak. Looking around here, I think the men who are doing the best have come off the farm. They're used to long hours and hard work.

We have finally finished our indoor work on the Link Trainers, machines with instruments and controls that simulate airplane cockpits. I know our instructors are hoping we will get all our mistakes out of our system now without hurting ourselves or anyone else and without damaging any of the government's precious airplanes. The country needs every airplane it has right now and can't afford to waste any on us dodos. Practice has only made me more excited than ever about finally getting up in a real BT-9. It has a blue fuselage and a single set of yellow wings. This is a big airfield, and there are hundreds of BT-9s and BT-14s here be-

cause the Army Air Forces needs to train thousands of pilots in order to win this war. If you didn't know better, and were looking down from the clouds, you'd think this field was covered by brightly colored butterflies.

I'm not ashamed to say that I was a little afraid the first few times I went up, but I am gaining confidence and think I'll be able to fly one of these things soon. I'm seeing everything from a whole new perspective up there. You would not believe how big the Earth seems, and also how fragile. I am more committed than ever to winning this war, and I know you will do whatever you can to help win it for us.

Grandma says that Grandpa has taught you to shoot a rifle. Every farm boy should know how to use a rifle. Just be careful. And how are the ducks? Did they hatch?

I know you're getting too big to hug, but if I could see you now, that is what I would do. Be good and help Grandma and Grandpa all you can.

Love,
Dad

When Gus finished reading the letters through a second time, he folded them and slid them back into their envelopes. Then he tucked them into the space behind the rafter where a small collection was accumulating. That pile felt to Gus as if it were a weight on his heart. Up until several weeks ago, he had never written to his parents; he'd had no need. His small family had simply never been apart before. The one time his father had taken a business trip to New York City, he'd sent Gus a penny post card filled with notes about the places he'd gone and the things he'd seen, such as the almost-brand-new Empire State Building, the tallest building in the world. Gus treasured the post card and kept it pressed flat in a dictionary at home, but it wasn't the message that made the card special; it was more that it was from his dad.

All these letters and post cards flying now around the country to Texas and the Adirondacks and Miller's Run were not friendly notes being sent for fun. They were more like fragile threads binding his family together despite the forces of war and sickness that threatened to sever them and send Gus, his father, and his mother spinning out beyond each other's reach. The letters meant more to him than the ducks, but the ducks evoked only feelings of love and tenderness. Looking at the growing pile of letters made him ache inside for everything that was missing and lost.

After Gus secured the letters, he climbed down the ladder and went into the house to get his grandfather's .30-30. Then he went out into the field behind the barn and walked through the grassy stubble to look at the circles he had drawn on the paper targets. He lay the rifle in the grass and pulled a short pencil from his back pocket. He couldn't figure out why his grandparents didn't like the Lavictoires, who had never done anything to them and who looked sort of like them, only poorer, which was hardly their fault. He drew a pair of slanted, almond-shaped eyes in the circles, like those on the Japanese faces he had seen in *Life* magazine, and after that he drew a nose and underneath that he blackened in a short mustache that looked like a woolly caterpillar. That's who I hate, he thought, Hirohito and Hitler and everyone else who has driven my family apart and scattered them to the far corners of creation. He picked up the rifle and paced off a safe shooting distance. Then he chambered a cartridge and leveled the barrel at the targets. Looking at the faces was unnerving, but he opened his eyes wide and stared at the mustache and squeezed the trigger. He chambered another cartridge and pulled the trigger again. Ten minutes later, the feed sacks were no more than tatters of cloth draped around singed hay. He stood there a minute breathing in deeply the sharp odor of gunpowder. Then he went down to the barn, cleaned the rifle, and put it away in the mudroom before he went into the kitchen for dinner.

Louise usually arrived just as dinner ended after walking the two miles down Cherry Hill and then up the hill to the Amslers'.

On hot days, Gus's grandmother had said it was okay for her to come into the kitchen—but no farther—for a glass of cold water. Louise seemed as shocked by the cleanliness of the Amslers' kitchen as Gus had been at the filth of the Lavictoires', and she was always on her best behavior with Gus's grandmother: *Please. Thank you, ma'am. No, thank you, ma'am. How are you today?*

"I want to name them," Louise said one day as she and Gus headed from the kitchen out to the barn.

"They're ducks," Gus protested. He had agreed to name Babe because Louise had persuaded him that the duckling couldn't get a proper burial without a name, but, in general, he didn't think ducks needed names.

"I know they're ducks," Louise said, "but I still think they need names. We named the other duck, the one that died."

"That was special," Gus said. "Because it died."

"Well, don't you think these ducks are special because they lived?"

With a sigh, Gus asked, "What do you want to name them?" They had reached the brooder and were looking down at the yellow fluffballs huddled under the brooder light. Gus imagined names like Alice and John, which were perfectly satisfactory names for people, but utterly silly names for ducks. Besides, the ducklings were still covered in soft yellow down. There was no way of knowing which were males and which were females—and according to his grandfather, that wouldn't change until they developed feathers.

"That one is Roosevelt, like the president of your country," Louise said, pointing to one duck that was slightly bigger than the others, "because it bosses the others around and chases them away from the food and water. That one is Louis, for Louis Armstrong, because it makes the most noise. That one is Fibber, for Fibber McGee. Do you see how its beak turns up a little? It sort of looks like it's smiling. And that one"—she pointed to the little duck with the crooked foot—"is Candy."

"Candy?" Gus broke out laughing. "What made you think of that?"

"Because it is little and sweet and it will never be mine," Louise said.

That shut Gus up. Now he took a moment to study Louise. She was dirty, for sure, but she was smart, too. She was also awfully skinny. He could see her bony knees right through her overalls, and her elbows were nothing but swollen knots of bone as big as his fist. Most kids he knew had round faces, but hers was long and narrow, with cheekbones that made her face look like she was sucking in her breath and holding it.

"Why isn't your father in the army?" he asked suddenly. He didn't know what made him say it. "My father is. Most all the men around here are if they're young enough to fight. The general store's plastered with signs saying 'Uncle Sam Wants You.' Seems like Uncle Sam would want your father, too."

"He has rickets, and he can't read," Louise said matter-of-factly.

"What are rickets?" Gus asked.

"I'm not sure, but it made his legs crooked," Louise said. "Besides, he can't read."

"English?" Gus asked. If the United States was fighting to liberate France, he thought there might be some use for men who could speak and write French.

"Anything," Louise said. "He can't read anything, not even his own name. Nobody ever taught him."

"But what if he needs to read something?" Gus asked in astonishment. "I don't know—like something at the store."

"I read it for him," Louise said. "He calls me his *cher bras droit*. That's his 'dear right hand,' but I'm more than a hand. I'm his eyes and ears, too."

Gus took Louise home that afternoon on his bicycle and was pleased that he could ride farther up the hill that climbed toward her house than he had been able to the previous week. Only once did she have to get off and walk beside him. He dropped her off in the front yard, where her little brothers and sisters were running around half naked and screaming like a bunch of banshees.

"What are rickets?" Gus asked his grandparents at supper that night.

"It's a vitamin deficiency," his grandmother explained. "People used to get it when I was little. It comes from too few vitamins and not enough sunshine. Why do you ask?"

"Louise says her father's not in the army because he has rickets," Gus said. He pointed to the carrots, and his grandmother gently swatted his hand.

"Nobody in this house points to the food they want," she admonished him. "If you want something passed to you, you ask for it."

"Please pass the carrots," Gus said sheepishly.

His grandfather handed him the bowl and winked at him.

"I wondered about that myself," his grandfather said. "Seems that most every able-bodied man in Miller's Run— for that matter, in the whole country—is in the army or working for the war effort except him. Same's true in Canada. Of course, some farmers get to stay home. Somebody's got to grow the food. But about all his place looks like it could grow is weeds."

"Louise says his legs aren't straight," Gus said.

"Yes, that's what rickets does," his grandmother said. "It

makes your bones soft so they bend. I knew a man with rickets when I was growing up. His legs were so bowed my mother used to say you could drive a team of horses through them. Come to think of it, he was a Quebecer, too. I can't imagine why the pope thinks people should have lots of babies if they can't feed them properly and keep their legs straight. Louise looks so thin that I imagine she's hardly getting enough to eat."

Gus was thinking the same thing.

After supper, he helped his grandmother wash and dry the dishes. Then he went into the living room and lay down in front of the radio. At six forty-five each evening Gus and his grandfather tuned in to CBS's *The World Today*. Gus always pulled a torn map of the world from the shelf below the radio so he could follow the war action while his grandfather took up his position on his back on the couch.

Gus found the war so complicated these days that he had trouble keeping everything straight, even with the help of the map. Major General "Tooey" Spaatz, whose name Gus loved to say, was an American commander in England. He was overseeing troops getting English airfields ready for American fighter and bomber pilots to arrive and start fighting the Nazis to regain control of the English Channel. Meanwhile, battleships, aircraft carriers, cruisers, destroyers, submarines, and transport ships were taking back islands from the Japanese in the southwestern Pacific. In Russia, the Germans were rolling toward the Black Sea, and the Red Army was igniting its own oil fields to keep them out of Nazi hands.

While he kept one ear tuned to the radio and one eye on

the map, Gus took an issue of *Life* off the magazine pile and started flipping through it. *Life* was one of two magazines the Amslers received. The other one was for his grandmother. It was a ladies' magazine that came every month and was filled with household tips and recipes like how to fix potatoes ten different ways. But *Life* came every week. It had something for everybody, including photographs of the war overseas. Gus pored over the black-and-white photographs of dead German soldiers and bombed-out munitions plants. He studied half-page advertisements for hit new movies like *Ten Gentlemen from West Point* that he would never see because Miller's Run didn't have a movie theater like the one he used to go to with his parents in Boston, and probably never would.

Suddenly, a large advertisement for Vimms vitamins caught his eye. According to the ad, three out of four Americans were vitamin-starved. The government had decreed that Americans should consume six different vitamins and three different minerals every day. Vimms offered vitamins A, B_1, B_2, C, D, and P-P, plus calcium, iron, and phosphorous. Gus didn't know which vitamin was responsible for preventing rickets, but he figured it had to be one that the government recommended, or else every American would be in danger of walking around with legs so crooked you could drive a team of horses through them. That wouldn't be good for the war effort or anything else. He read the ad carefully. Vimms promised to make people who are weary and tired feel sharp and alive. He read the prices: twenty-four tablets for fifty cents or ninety-six tablets for $1.75. That was expensive! He'd been picking potato bugs for three weeks now, and he had only thirteen cents. Of course, he didn't pick every bug he saw. Sometimes, he was hardly paying attention at all. More than once, his grandmother had gone out into the garden after he had supposedly done his job and, before moving three steps, found a dozen beetles. She'd let him know, too.

His eyes roved over the magazine's photographs of cute children and shipbuilding plants, and he scoured the ads. He found one for Ovaltine, and immediately he perked up. His grandmother kept Ovaltine in her cupboard. "If you awaken tired or nerve-jangled—if your freshness and sparkle are slipping," the ad read, "you should know this: New, improved Ovaltine has vitamins and minerals. Use it night and morning. See if you don't begin to sleep better and awaken feeling and looking fresh and buoyant."

Buoyant, Gus thought, now that would be something. He was getting plenty of fresh air and sunshine, and his grandmother fed him so well you'd hardly know there was a war going on, but still, he couldn't say he felt *buoyant*. Imagine being able to just float through your day. He lifted one of his arms and tried to imagine it hanging in the air, suspended without any effort on his part. Vitamins were starting to look more and more interesting.

He also found an ad for Carnation unsweetened evaporated milk. "Just add water," it read. "It gives a girl GO when she EATS her milk!" But the promotion didn't stop there. The ad suggested "partifying" the milk to make it practically irresistible, and it drove that point home by including a recipe for cherry Bavarian cream pie using Carnation evaporated milk. The pie looked pretty good to Gus, even though he was a boy with plenty of go already. All these ads were getting him thinking.

Suddenly, he realized that his radio program was almost over and he'd missed most of it.

"When that show's finished, Gus, we'll head out," his grandfather said, waking up from his after-supper nap on the couch. He shook out the weekly newspaper as if he'd really been reading it and not just sleeping underneath it. Then he stood up and stretched.

Gus put the magazine on top of the pile of other issues of *Life*, so that he could refer to it later, and went outside.

The sky was half filled with clouds, and the air was cool. Tonight, Gus knew, it would be important to listen carefully, because a German zeppelin could pass directly overhead, above the cloud cover, without being seen. He sat beside his grandfather without saying anything and wished he had worn his sweater. At first, all they heard was the plaintive call of a whippoorwill singing in the woods beyond the fields. Later, they heard, as they always did, the sharp cries of bats and the endless whine of night insects, but otherwise the night was as still and silent as a church the day after Christmas. The next farm was half a mile away, and some nights, when the wind was right and they were sitting on the benches in the old playhouse with their ears tuned for the distant throb of an airplane, they could hear the mooing of a cow, but not tonight.

"Your father sounds happy enough, though he misses you and your mother something dreadful," Gus's grandfather said after a while. He was smoking again, and the comforting glow of the pipe bowl illuminated his rough face. "I think he's taken a liking to flying."

"I miss him a lot," Gus said, but he regretted the words as soon as he spoke them. Maybe he had hurt his grandfather's feelings. "I *am* having fun here," he assured his grandfather. And he was—much more than he had expected to when he boarded the train in Boston in June. He had the ducklings, and they were thriving, growing every day, even the one with the bad foot. He had learned to shoot a rifle and could hit the target now from thirty or forty yards. He had Louise.

"It's okay to miss your mother and father, lad," his grandfather said and patted Gus's knee in the dark. "Let's just keep hoping that this arrangement is temporary and has a happy ending."

Chapter Six

Two weeks after they hatched, the ducklings finally started to look like ducks. They were still covered with yellow down, but the brown patches had spread, almost like creeping shadows, outlining their wings and running in stripes back from their eyes and across their backs. Their wings were beginning to look like real wings, although they were still ridiculously small and stubby. Whenever the ducklings stretched to their full height and flapped their wings, pretending that they had big plans of going somewhere, Gus had to laugh. They couldn't fly any higher than Gus could by flapping his arms. When they pipped, as they often did because they seemed to have a lot to say, he sometimes thought he heard the beginning of a quack, but it might have been just a sneeze.

Gus came into the barn every morning cooing, "Hey, ducks." The ducklings immediately set up a racket, but it wasn't the terrified crying of the first few days. Now it was a greeting. All four of the ducks waddled over to the water jar and the meal dish and waited impatiently, like small children eager to meet Santa Claus. Gus continued to speak to them softly, and they moved easily around his hands in the brooder as he went about his business. But he had to admit that his grandfather had known what he was talking about. They sure weren't kittens. If Gus reached for any one of them to pet it or pick it up, it broadcast a loud warning and set all the other ducklings fleeing for the comfort of the brooder light, where their small, beady eyes regarded him as if he had broken some sacred trust.

Candy was still the smallest duckling. To his surprise and in spite of himself, he had grown comfortable calling the ducks by the names Louise had given them. But enough was enough. Yesterday, Louise had arrived with pictures she had cut out of the Sears, Roebuck catalog.

"What are those for?" Gus had asked.

"The ducks have nothing to look at. They're bored. Look at them," Louise explained.

She marched over to the workbench and grabbed a hammer. Then she fished around in the saucers of odds and ends until she had half a dozen small nails. She hammered the nails into the inside walls of the brooder while the ducks scurried to a far corner and gabbled nervously, as if the sky were falling in on them. Afterward, she hung her pictures on the nails. Then she stood up to admire her decorating.

Gus leaned over to take a look. One was an illustration of a tractor. Another was an advertisement showing a woman modeling a dress. One was an illustration of a child sporting new shoes. Two more were drawings of other kinds of farm machinery, and the last one was an advertisement of a man in overalls.

As the ducklings calmed down, they ventured out to examine the new décor. Two of them pecked at the pictures, trying to see if they could eat them. When all they got for their trouble was newsprint, they quickly lost interest and waddled back to the duck meal.

"They like them," Louise said.

Gus rolled his eyes. He had bigger troubles. The second bag of meal was nearly gone. Within a week, he would have to let the ducklings loose in the barnyard to scratch for insects and grass. He wasn't sure they were ready to make it on their own.

After breakfast every morning, Gus checked on the ducks and then went immediately out to the Victory Garden. All the plants were doing their part, coming along well. Rain fell regularly, usually at night, and everything in the garden was flourishing. As long as he avoided touching the beans, which his grandma said would catch some dreadful disease if they were touched while wet, he preferred working in the morning, when the soil was damp. Weeds could be pulled up easily. The potato beetles and bean caterpillars were sluggish after a night of gorging on the plants. Gus picked them off, every one, and flicked them into the kerosene. He had twenty cents in his top drawer.

Louise hadn't been around since decorating the brooder. Just when he had started hinting to his grandmother how much Louise might like a glass of Ovaltine the next time she visited—part of his plan to help her look fresh and feel buoyant—she had stopped coming. He was afraid that he was too late. Maybe she'd already come down with rickets.

"Can I go over to Louise's?" he asked when he came in from the garden one morning.

"'May I?'" his grandmother reminded him. "Are your chores done?" She pushed her glasses into place and peered down into the can Gus was holding. "That's a good penny's worth," she admitted. She went over to a crock on the kitchen counter where she kept the money she earned from selling her chickens' eggs, lifted the lid, and shoved in her hand up to her wrist. Gus could hear the jangle of coins as she rummaged around. Finally, she withdrew her hand, holding a penny in her fingers. She handed it to him. "You're getting to be quite a wealthy young man. What are you saving up for?"

"Something special. I'll tell you later," he said. Not yet, but he knew he would have to tell her at some point, because it was too far to ride his bike all the way to the general store. "And yes, my chores are done. At least, everything for this morning."

That was the way things were on the farm. Nothing was ever really finished. Tonight the ducklings would need more fresh water and meal. The pig would need her slops, although his bucket was lighter these days now that the piglets had been sold to other farmers. If his grandmother hadn't gotten around to tending her chickens, Gus would have to take care of them, too, but the day was otherwise free. That was one advantage of having the cows gone. Gus's grandfather could make up for all the sleep he'd lost over the years by getting up at four-thirty, and Gus had free time on his hands.

"I guess you may go," she agreed. "I'll be going down-

street to the village with your grandfather as soon as I get the
dishes cleaned up from dinner."

Gus hadn't expected his grandmother to take a trip to the village so soon and he changed his plans on the spot. He waited
in his room until he heard his grandmother slowly making her
way up the stairs. On the bed in front of him, he had spread
out twenty-one pennies. It was all the money he had in the
world, but it was not enough to buy even a small box of
Vimms. Just considering what he was about to do made his
face burn. If his parents knew his intentions, he was pretty
sure they'd be so ashamed of him that he wouldn't be able to
look them in the eye.

As soon as he heard the door to his grandparents' bedroom close, he pocketed the pennies and eased his door open.
He stole down the stairs, keeping close to the wall to avoid the
creaks and groans of the old boards. In the kitchen, he lifted
the lid off the crock where his grandmother kept her egg
money and reached in. It made him sick to be stealing from
his grandmother; even more disheartening was how easy it
was. She was so trusting that she kept all the ready cash she
had out in the open in her kitchen. Gus counted out twenty-
nine cents, all in pennies, so she would never wonder where
on earth he had gotten his hands on a dime. Then he carefully
replaced the lid and went and sat on the front stoop.

Ten minutes later, his grandmother and grandfather
came out, headed for the truck. His grandmother was pin-
ning her hat into place.

"Would you get me something, Grandma?" Gus blurted

out as he jumped off the stoop and startled them. His grandfather sensed that this had nothing to do with him, and he continuing hobbling toward the truck.

"I knew it. All that potato bug money burning a hole in your overall pockets?" Gus's grandmother laughed.

"I have fifty cents here," he explained, his face so hot and red he felt certain that he must be on the verge of dying of heat stroke.

"Fifty cents! Just think," his grandmother exclaimed, "every penny of it earned on your knees. My old back is grateful for your help, young man. You've earned a treat. What would you like for that fifty cents?"

"I want some Vimms vitamins," Gus said. "They're twenty-four tablets for fifty cents."

"Don't you think you're getting enough vitamins?" His grandmother studied him closely. "Are you feeling poorly? You look awfully flushed. Let me see your eyes."

"They're not for me," he said, shuffling backward, trying to avoid her scrutiny.

"Well, then, who are they for?"

"They're for Louise," he said, looking at his feet. "I don't want her to get rickets."

"Louise!" his grandmother said. "Well, there's no denying that she's a scrawny-looking thing. I don't suppose a few vitamins would hurt her, but that's a mighty generous thing for you to do with your hard-earned money."

"Just get them, Grandma, please," Gus begged. "If you saw her house, you'd understand."

"I understand *without* seeing her house," his grandmother

said. "That's something I have no intention of seeing. But I like the girl. She's filthy and she needs a good bath, but there's something appealing about her. I'll get the Vimms."

After the truck disappeared down the hill, Gus rode the bike over to the Lavictoires'. He'd read in the newspaper just yesterday that the country was cutting down on bike production in order to save metal for war-related items like tanks and planes. He felt lucky that his grandfather never threw anything away. Why would he, with a whole big barn to fill? That barn was like a treasure chest, full of everything a person needed.

He could hear the commotion at the Lavictoires' even before he crested the hill. The whole family was out in the fields behind the house. They were haying. Gus recognized Mr. Lavictoire by his bandy legs, which bowed out so far that he thought the man could walk on his knees if he ever needed to. He was standing ankle-deep in field stubble and pitching hay high atop a horse-drawn wagon. He stooped to fork the hay and then swung the tumble, a pile of it nearly as big as he was, high over his head in a graceful arc. The forkful settled like falling snow onto the load of golden hay that was already as big as a boat and threatening to swamp the wagon. Louise, André, and Henri were perched on top, balancing like circus performers. They grabbed the pitched hay and used their own forks to settle it so it wouldn't slide off. Mrs. Lavictoire was up front, sitting on the narrow wagon seat and driving a nag that looked like it just wanted to lie down and die. The smallest Lavictoires were running around underfoot while their father shouted at them in such a coarse and gruff way that Gus wondered if he was swearing at them.

The air was thick with chaff, which swirled around as if it were a storm brewing.

Gus stood at the edge of the field and watched for several minutes. Then Louise raised her head and saw him. She grinned and waved, but in those few seconds her father pitched a forkful of hay in her direction and knocked her over. Except for her feet, she disappeared into the soft mountain beneath her. Mr. Lavictoire glanced over his shoulder to see what had caught his daughter's attention and motioned for Gus to come closer. Hesitantly, Gus parked his bike against a stump and walked in the direction of the hay wagon.

Mr. Lavictoire limped toward him over a rough field of cut hay that reminded Gus of his own crewcut. Mr. Lavictoire's face was blackened with dirt and sweat, except around his eyes, where the sockets were pale with fatigue. Hay stuck out of his black hair and made him look like the scarecrow in Gus's grandmother's garden. He used the handle of his pitchfork to help him keep his balance over the uneven ground. Watching him approach with his pitchfork didn't fill Gus with confidence. Louise jumped down from the wagon, a good eight feet, and landed gracefully on her feet, as if she were used to these high-wire acts. Then she sprinted to join her father. All the little children quieted down and waited, just the way the ducklings would have. Mrs. Lavictoire slumped in her seat and lowered her head. She looked as though she felt the same way the horse did.

"Té-tu capable de mener la wagune à quatre roues?" Mr. Lavictoire said when he reached Gus.

"He wants to know if you can drive a wagon," Louise said, catching up with them. "Mama isn't feeling good."

"Facile, le chevau sait quoi faire," Mr. Lavictoire said. He made a pushing motion with his free hand, then flipped it palm side up and shrugged.

"He says it's easy. The horse knows what to do," Louise said.

"It looks harder than that," Gus said doubtfully. He didn't know anything about driving a horse or pulling a wagon, even if it appeared that the horse wasn't any more capable of running away with the wagon than he was.

"It's easy," Louise assured him. "The horse hardly moves."

They all turned toward the wagon. Mrs. Lavictoire had already decided things for everyone. She was climbing awkwardly off the wagon seat, and when she reached the ground, Gus could see that she would soon be having another baby. Without paying them any mind, she turned and lumbered toward the house, one hand held to her swollen stomach. The horse stood by patiently, even though no one was holding the reins. Its head sagged almost to the ground.

Gus crossed the field of dry hay and climbed onto the wagon seat. Then he took up the reins and glanced around for someone to tell him what to do. Mr. Lavictoire made a shaking motion with his hands. "Git!"

Gus shook the reins and the horse took one step, then another and another. Louise jumped aboard the wagon and climbed to the crown of the hay. Mr. Lavictoire smiled encouragingly at Gus and forked some hay high up to his children. They went to work.

This became the longest afternoon Gus had ever known. He grew familiar with every knot and imperfection in the wagon seat. His back ached. The air was too thick with chaff to breathe. They made two trips to the barn with loads of hay that looked like small mountains. Everyone worked to unload the hay into the mow, and then they headed out to the field again. The horse plodded along, already well acquainted with the routine and too exhausted to protest the effort it took to keep itself and the bony milk cow fed next winter.

But there was no stopping. Clouds were moving in, and even Gus, a city boy, had spent enough time in the country to know that hay couldn't get wet before it was put up or it would rot and spoil. The children struggled to keep up. Mr. Lavictoire barked orders at them until he began to sound like an angry dog, but every time he turned toward Gus, he smiled his gap-toothed smile and nodded his head encouragingly. Louise seemed tireless until the last hour, when she looked as though she was having trouble staying on her feet on top of the gigantic pile of hay. Gus began to worry that she would fall.

As Gus was walking out of the barn and the last loads were being forked into the hayloft, he saw a whirlwind coming up the road. His grandfather's truck pulled into the Lavictoires' short driveway and stopped. The engine died and dust settled over the fading paint. His grandfather leaned out the window.

"Your grandmother is worried sick," he said. "We waited supper and you didn't come home. She asked me to come fetch you. All I can say is that you'd better have a pretty good excuse for your tomfoolery, because I just used rationed gas driving over here to get you when you could have used your own two good legs to get home."

"We've been haying, Grandpa," Gus explained.

"What do you mean, you've been haying?" his grandfather asked. He studied Gus, who looked like one of the Lavictoires now, with his scarecrow hair and dirty face. "Where's the crew?"

"We were it," Gus said. "The Lavictoires and me."

"You mean you and those scrawny kids brought in a field of hay?" his grandfather asked in disbelief.

"And Mr. Lavictoire," Gus added. "He pitched all the hay. Louise did most of the loading. I drove."

Gus's grandfather considered Gus and the children running loose in the field as if this was all beyond his understanding. He turned his attention to Louise's father and studied him as he used a horse fork to swing the last load of hay high over his head into the barn loft. Then he took off his hat and wiped his forearm across his forehead. "Well, I'll be. Don't that beat all."

Gus's grandfather was still leaning out his truck window looking surprised when Mr. Lavictoire hobbled over. He nodded, and Gus's grandfather returned the nod. Neither man spoke or smiled. Then Mr. Lavictoire held out his hand toward Gus, offering a dime in fingers so dirty they might as well have been made from the earth itself. *"Merci,"* he said.

Gus didn't move. A dime was a lot of money, and he thought of the Captain America comic book he could buy with that dime now that he had arranged to get some vitamins for Louise. Of course, what he should do with it was slip it into the crock where his grandmother kept her egg money, to replace some of what he'd stolen. That dime was worth ten cans of beetles, one third of what he'd stolen. It would go a ways toward assuaging his conscience, which burned in him like a July afternoon. But he figured accepting the money from Mr. Lavictoire meant one more thing his family couldn't afford, and they were already doing without plenty—everything from food to soap to clothes.

He barely smiled and shook his head. Mr. Lavictoire didn't press. He pocketed the dime in his grubby overalls and shifted uncomfortably. Then he stuck out his hand. Gus took Mr. Lavictoire's gnarled, dirty hand and shook it, surprised at how filthy his own hand was after the afternoon's work.

"Hurry up, Gus," his grandfather urged. "Put your bike in the truck. Your grandmother is waiting on us."

Neither Gus nor his grandfather said anything until they were at the bottom of Cherry Hill and starting up the road toward home.

"That man has a talent for a pitchfork," Gus's grandfather said.

Gus turned and glanced at his grandfather but didn't say anything. Both were silent the rest of the way home, but as soon as Gus came into the kitchen, the silence ended.

"Mercy me," Gus's grandma exclaimed. "Look at you!

You can tell me what happened later, but right now you are going to get out of my kitchen and clean yourself up."

Later, over supper, Gus told his grandparents about haying, but not before he'd eaten six of his grandmother's rolls. Every one of them was slathered in strawberry jam she'd put up just a few weeks earlier, when the berries were so full and ripe they lay in the bed beside the house like red eggs.

"You can spare me the details about the haying," his grandfather said. "I've put up enough hay in my life to carpet the state of Vermont. And I did most of it the way you did— by hand, with horses. But I'm impressed that you and a straggly bunch of children managed it. It's a man's work, it's hard, and it's dirty. It's darn near impossible to run a farm without help. I know. I've done that, too, and it almost killed me."

Afterward, they talked about the weather. A storm was moving in. They could hear thunder rolling in from someplace far away. Out beyond the garden, the leaves of the apple trees flipped their pale green undersides skyward like circus dancers Gus had seen a year ago, tossing their skirts so high he had laughed at how scandalized his mother pretended to be. The air was green and close. Humidity clung to their clothes and stuck them to their chairs where they sat. Gus thought of all the hay the Lavictoires would have lost if they hadn't gotten it safely into the barn this day.

When the storm finally struck, thunder echoed up and down the valley. Rain came down in torrents, pelting the house and streaking the windows. Gus's grandmother stood by the kitchen sink and tried to see if her garden was floating away, but all she could glimpse in the dizzying flashes of light was the scarecrow looking like a bedraggled hobo wandering in the night.

"I did your ducks for you," Gus's grandfather said when the storm had ebbed. "And the pig. You can go to bed. You've earned your rest."

Gus couldn't say how grateful he was. Although he had mostly sat while others, including a girl, did the hard labor, he was so tired that he ached in every bone. He fell asleep before the last peal of thunder rolled away over the hills to the east.

———

"Get up!" Gus heard his grandfather say. "Gus, get up!"

He was still exhausted, and he opened his eyes slowly, unsure of himself and where he was. His grandfather nudged his shoulder.

"Something's after your ducks," his grandfather said. "I think it's got one already, but it'll be back for another."

Gus sat up sharply, as if someone had slapped him.

"Get a move on, son. Put some pants on," his grandfather said.

For the first time, Gus noticed that his grandfather was carrying a rifle, the .22.

"What are we going to do?" Gus asked. He could feel his heart pounding.

"I'm going to hold the flashlight, and you're going to shoot it, whatever it is, fox or raccoon—probably a raccoon," his grandfather said.

"Shoot it?" Gus asked stupidly.

"Shoot it," his grandfather repeated. "If you don't, it will keep coming back until it's killed every one of those ducks you've been working so hard to raise."

"I can't shoot it," Gus protested, dancing on one foot and struggling to get his second leg into his overalls. He was also trying to come fully awake as the idea of taking aim at something other than a bag of hay settled in his brain. He was horrified at the thought of killing something, even if it was to protect his ducklings. Besides, he wasn't sure he could shoot straight enough to kill anything that moved—he'd been practicing on feedbags.

"Why don't *you* shoot it?" he asked his grandfather as he hooked the straps on his overalls.

"I don't trust myself to use a gun at night anymore. I might take out a window or I might kill the ducks. Hell, I could miss the whole barn in the dark," his grandfather said. "Come on, hurry up. You're giving him time to come back for seconds."

They could tell even with the big doors closed that the ducklings were riled up. They gabbled and quacked and sounded frightened, the way they used to when Gus rushed into the barn without thinking and without giving them time to adjust to his arrival. His own breathing quickened just listening to them.

Gus and his grandfather waited in the dark about twenty yards from the barn. The rifle felt cool and deadly in his hand, lighter than the .30-30. They stood there a good ten minutes before they heard rustling, and another minute before they had a good idea of where the soft, whispering sound was coming from. Gus pointed, and his grandfather snapped on the flashlight, aiming it at a broken window above one of the barn's old horse stalls. A fat raccoon froze in the spotlight, the dark mask on its face turned back toward them in surprise and its bushy striped tail hanging down from where it was poised in the window frame.

"Shoot it, Gus!" his grandfather ordered.

Gus raised the rifle into place. The butt found that sweet spot against his shoulder where it had grown comfortable, and his left arm stretched down the barrel, his hand tight around the cool metal. Then he froze.

His finger felt numb on the trigger. "I can't, Grandpa," Gus whimpered. The barrel of the rifle began to bounce with his dry sobs.

"Shoot it, Gus!" his grandfather ordered. "If you don't, that raccoon won't stop until it's killed every one of your precious ducks."

Gus held his breath, took aim, and fired.

"That's my boy!" his grandfather said, raising his arm higher so the flashlight threw a wide arc of light. "You got it with one shot, son."

Gus couldn't look. He dropped the rifle in the wet grass and ran to pull open the barn doors. Inside, he flicked on the lights. The ducks were quacking excitedly, running frantically around the brooder and beating their immature wings against the wooden sides as if they could fly if only they tried hard enough. Gus saw immediately that one duckling was missing. That made him frantic, too. He ran wherever the light reached in the cavernous barn, but all he found were drops of blood on some straw in a manger near the broken window where the raccoon had perched.

His grandfather came into the barn holding the dead raccoon by its tail. Blood ran down the fur on one side and dripped on the barn floor.

"Oh, Grandpa," Gus wailed. "He killed one."

"I was afraid of that when I heard all the racket being kicked up out here. It's a good thing your grandmother opened the bedroom window after the storm passed," Gus's grandfather said. "That raccoon would have killed more of your ducks, maybe all of them, if you hadn't shot it. I'm sorry, but that's the way things work. Those coons, they kill for the sheer sport of it.

"Get the gun and bring it in here," his grandfather instructed him. "The wet grass will ruin it. Then go on inside and back to bed. The ducks will quiet down if we leave them alone. Tell your grandmother I'm going to skin the coon before I come in, and then I'm going to clean the gun. She ought to go along to bed."

Inside, Gus lay sleepless under the sheet in the night's muggy stillness. His mind raced with images of blood dripping from the raccoon's mouth as it hung by his grandfather's side and the memory of blood dappling the straw in the horse stall where the raccoon had dragged his duckling through the window. He hoped it had died quickly and hadn't suffered. He tried to figure out whether it was Roosevelt, Louis, or Fibber who had died, but he had been too upset to study the ducklings carefully, and they'd been too upset to stay still so he could get a good look at them. He'd seen Candy's crooked foot, so he knew it wasn't her, and he was surprisingly relieved. Until that moment, he hadn't known he had a favorite. But the loss still hurt deeply. He thought of the power of the rifle as it jerked against his shoulder, and he reached to touch his bare skin where even now it tingled.

This was the third worst day of his life, after the day his father left for Texas and the day his mother left for the Adirondacks. It had begun with him stealing from his grandmother and had ended with him killing another living being. He thought about the minister of his church back in Boston, standing in front of the congregation in his black vestments, with his arms raised like angel wings as he addressed what he called his flock about the wages of sin and the terrors of hell. At least he didn't have to face that image in Miller's Run, where the church had been shuttered tight ever since the minister enlisted last March.

Still, Gus knew that regardless of all the good things he had done in his short life—set the table, or shoveled the front walk without being asked, or helped the Lavictoires with their haying—that he'd broken two of the Ten Commandments today and hell was in his future now. Perhaps to punish him, God would make sure he never again saw his parents in this life, and he would most certainly not see them in the next. Unlike him, they were too good to be sent to hell. His heart felt small and tight in his chest, as if someone had tied it up with baling twine. And yet he could not help thinking about how small his own flock was now and how sick Louise might be, and he lay awake a long time with his mind too full to sleep.

Chapter Seven

"It's time to let 'em go," Gus's grandfather said over breakfast the next morning.

"Let who go?" Gus's grandmother asked as she bustled from the stove to the table carrying a skillet full of fried potatoes and onions.

Gus knew who. It was the morning after the raccoon attack. He was exhausted and angry and sad all at once, and he didn't have to ask. He put a potato in his mouth and chewed slowly.

"The ducks," his grandfather explained. "It's time they learned to fend for themselves. They're too helpless penned up in that brooder in the barn. Besides, the meal is almost gone, isn't it, Gus?"

Gus nodded miserably. The flock had shrunk from seven eggs to three frightened ducklings. He had lost faith in his ability to keep the remaining ducklings safe, but he thought that freeing them from the brooder would only make things worse. He just couldn't bring himself to say so.

"Well, then, let's do it. I'll meet you in the barn in half an hour," Gus's grandfather said. He pushed back his chair from the table.

"Wait," Gus said. "I want to go get Louise. She'd like to see them let loose."

A heavy silence fell over the room as Gus's grandparents looked at each other.

"Louise isn't welcome here anymore," his grandmother said finally.

"Why not?" Gus looked from one grandparent to the other as if his head were a weathervane finding direction in a rough wind.

"I'm sorry," his grandmother said, "but I warned you from the start that those Quebecers couldn't be trusted to cross a room without stealing something, even if it's only a glance."

"That's true, son," his grandfather agreed. "Seems they haven't changed one bit since I was your age."

"What's missing?" Gus asked. He couldn't imagine Louise stealing anything, not even a green bean.

"There's twenty-nine cents of my egg money gone. I know how much money I had in there, because I was saving up for a new oilcloth for the table. But it's not there now. And since I know your grandfather hasn't taken one penny of my egg money in sixty years of marriage, and I know you would never steal, that leaves only Louise. It was probably a mistake to invite her into the kitchen. Just too much temptation. I'm sorry, Gus, but you can't say we didn't warn you."

Gus's grandmother came over and started clearing away

the salt and pepper and strawberry jam. She put her hand gently on Gus's back.

"I have what you asked for, though," she said. She went over to the crock on the counter where she kept her money and reached inside. When she pulled her hand out, she was gripping a small paper package that read "Vimms."

"Never mind that she took advantage of our hospitality. Maybe you can ride over to the Lavictoires' sometime today or tomorrow and give this to Louise. I may be waiting for the day when she and her family go back where they came from, but that doesn't mean I want her to get sick. It's not her fault that she comes from a long line of thieves and sneaks. But I won't have her around the place anymore."

Gus stumbled from the room, his face the color of fireplace ash. Up in his bedroom he closed the door and sat on the bed. He opened the package of Vimms and poured three of the pills into his hand. They were small and round, like peas, but white, and he found it difficult to believe that each one contained six vitamins plus calcium, phosphorous, and iron. Just what *were* vitamins and how could anyone squeeze six of them and three minerals into such a little pill? But at that moment, he could not imagine anyone feeling worse than he did. Even though it only added to his sense of guilt, he put one of the pills on his tongue. When it started to dissolve, he began gagging, but he gathered up the saliva in his mouth and swallowed hard. The pill stuck in his throat, and he had to swallow over and over to wash it down. He sat on the bed and waited for the vitamin to make him feel better. Twice as alive was probably too much to ask for, but maybe it would help him feel a little stronger, strong enough to face up to everything he'd done.

But there was no miracle cure. Instead, taking one of Louise's precious pills had only made him feel worse. He carefully rewrapped the rest of them and put the package in his overall pocket. Then he went and got a piece of paper and a pencil and wrote a letter to his father.

> *Dear Dad,*
>
> *I have done a terrible thing and I think the only reason I can bring myself to tell you is that you are far away so I won't have to see the look on your face. But now I need advice. And I need it quick. I have made a friend here. Her name is Louise Lavictoire, and as you have probably already figured out, she is a Quebecer. Nobody likes the Lavictoires, not even Grandma and Grandpa, because they are Catholic and different and speak French, but Louise is a good girl and my best friend. I read in a magazine that vitamins can help people get healthy, and Louise is awfully skinny, so I bought her some vitamins with the money I've saved from picking beetles and worms off the vegetables in Grandma's Victory Garden. But I didn't have enough money, so I took 29¢ of Grandma's egg money without asking her, and now Grandma thinks Louise took the money and won't let her come over anymore. Help me, please! I know that what I did is wrong, but I'm too afraid to admit to Grandma what I did because I'm afraid Grandma and Grandpa will tell me I have to leave. Please write back soon and tell me what to do. I know you are ashamed of me. I'm very sorry.*
>
> *Your son,*
>
> *Gus*

Gus went downstairs and found an envelope and a stamp and addressed the letter. He left it on the kitchen table, where his grandfather would find it and take it to town on his next trip. Then he headed out to the barn.

His grandfather was waiting, leaning against the door and chewing on his pipe. "That's too bad about Louise, but your grandmother warned you, Gus. Now, let's take a look at these ducks. Can't say as I blame them, but they're as spooked as a drunk in a graveyard," his grandfather said. "They're acting like they saw the devil himself last night."

Gus walked cautiously into the barn. As he approached the brooder, the ducks started raising a general alarm. They ran to the brooder light, as they always did when they were frightened, and huddled there, as if the light were more than warmth and brightness. They still acted like they believed the light somehow threw a halo of safety around them.

"Hey, ducks," Gus said softly. "Hey, ducks."

To Gus's surprise, the ducklings quieted down. They stood stiff and tense but they were willing to listen to him.

"Hey, ducks."

Gus lowered his hand into the brooder and picked up a handful of meal from the feeding dish. He studied the ducklings and decided that it was Fibber who had run out of luck and fallen victim to the raccoon.

The ducklings regarded him skeptically with their beady eyes for half a minute, and then waddled over and started pecking at his hand.

Behind him, Gus heard his grandfather chuckle. "I guess they know who their mama is," he said.

"Now what do we do?" Gus asked.

"Now we scare the Holy Ghost out of them by picking them up and putting them on the barn floor," his grandfather said. "Then we stand the brooder up in the corner over there. From now on, these ducks can bed down with the chickens in the coop. At least at night they'll be safe in there from the raccoons. And there's not much that's going to get them during the day, except a man with a gun."

Gus's grandfather was right about how skittish the ducks were after their ordeal with the raccoon. The second Gus started reaching for them, they retreated with much name calling to the far reaches of the brooder. Finally, his grandfather cut off their angles of escape and Gus was able to reach in and grab them one at a time and dump them unceremoniously on the barn floor. They acted as if their dignity had been wounded by such callous treatment, and they waddled about, shaking out their feathers and winding down their speeches.

"Now what?" Gus asked.

"I'll move the brooder, and you go do your chores in your grandmother's garden," his grandfather said.

Gus turned and headed toward the doorway. He figured the ducks would stay huddled in the barn. After all, the barn floor was the only ground they'd ever known; the barn rafters, the only sky. Instead, the ducks collected around his ankles like dust balls, tangling themselves up in his feet.

Stepping lightly, he led the parade out the barn door, across the yard, and right into his grandmother's garden, with his grandfather's laughter echoing in his ears. When he knelt and started gathering bugs and caterpillars, the ducks got to work, too. And to think he'd been worried they might not be able to fend for themselves! After a couple of minutes, he just sat back and watched. The ducklings had spread out among the plants and were pecking away, lifting leaves with their bills and clearing the foliage of every intruder they could find. At this rate, they were going to put him out of business. In half an hour, Gus had perhaps eighteen beetles in his can—a far sight less than a penny's worth—and the ducks were looking at him as if they were awaiting further instructions.

He was amazed at how quickly the thrill of their adulation wore off. He wanted to flap his arms at them and tell them to go find something to do, the way his mother sometimes shooed him out of the kitchen when she was cooking and he was trolling for something to snack on. But he knew that would frighten them. He'd spent his days being gentle and gaining their trust, and he wasn't going to ruin it the first time they left the barn. Still, he had something he needed to do now, and the ducks couldn't be a part of it. Asking his grandparents to baby-sit was out of the question. They'd made it clear the ducks were his responsibility.

Finally, Gus led them back to the barn and wheeled the bicycle out the doorway. Then he scraped around on the floor until he had gathered a small pile of abandoned feed. Now he had their complete attention, and they lined up in front of him like students attending their first day of school. Heaping more guilt onto his already stricken conscience, he threw the feed toward the water jar, and as soon as the ducks waddled off in search of it, he hurried out of the barn and slammed the doors closed behind him. Without waiting to hear their distress at discovering they had been conned, Gus climbed on the bike and took off down the hill.

At the Lavictoires', the children were tending the garden. Unlike his grandmother's Victory Garden, which was a flourishing green jungle of vegetables and foliage, this one looked as anemic as the children working in it. The tendrils of green beans twined around the thin branches stuck in the dirt as poles, but instead of looking robust, the beans looked undersized and fragile. The broccoli and cabbage had been overrun with worms, which the youngest Lavictoires were now plucking off and squishing with their bare feet. Louise and one of her brothers were thinning the carrots and onions, which had been allowed to grow too densely and were consequently half the size of his grandmother's. In the middle of all this, the scarecrow with the broken arms and the pale blue-flowered dress reigned, but her attitude was more one of despair than victory. This was not how the war was going to be won.

"Hi." Louise grinned at Gus as he wheeled the bike over beside the garden, but after she'd seen his face, her own darkened. "Are the ducks okay?"

"We had a little accident last night," Gus said.

"What? What happened?" Louise hopped over the vegetable rows until she was standing beside him, looking intently into his face. "Are they all right?"

"A raccoon got into the barn and killed one of them," Gus admitted. "It was awful. My grandpa woke me up in the middle of the night and made me go out to the barn with him with the rifle. When we saw the raccoon headed through a broken window, he made me shoot it."

Louise's eyes were huge. "Did you get it?"

"First shot," Gus said, proud in spite of himself.

"Who died?" Louise asked. "Not Candy—*please* not Candy."

"No," said Gus, "it was Fibber. . . . No more silly smiles."

Louise let out a big breath but she had tears in her eyes. "What're you going to do now?"

"Grandpa made me take 'em out of the brooder. He said they'd be safer during the day if they could fend for themselves, and we'll lock them up at night with the chickens."

"I wish you'd waited until I could've come up before letting them go. I'll bet it was pretty funny setting them loose." Louise smiled.

"Well, that's the thing," Gus said, his face turning red. "You can't come up for a while. Grandma's sick with some bug. She's afraid that if you come up, you'll catch it and bring it back here and give it to everyone else. She doesn't want your mom getting sick, what with the baby coming and all."

"I almost never get sick," Louise protested. Her disappointment was so obvious and so acute that Gus almost broke down and told her the truth, but by now he felt as if he had fallen into a pit of quicksand. About the only relief he could hope for was that a lightning bolt would come out of the sky and put him out of his misery.

"Here," he said, reaching into his overall pocket. "I bought these for you."

"Candy?" Louise asked, studying the paper covering.

"No, vitamins," Gus explained.

"What are vitamins?"

"I don't really know," Gus admitted. "I was reading in *Life* magazine about Vimms vitamins and how they help people stay healthy. Each pill has six different kinds of vitamins in it, plus phosphorous, iron, and calcium. I thought they might help you not get rickets, like your dad." He did not mention that the advertisement promised more. It guaranteed Vimms would make the person taking them feel vigorous and more alive. He himself had yet to feel any effect whatsoever from the pill he had taken a little earlier, so he didn't want to promise anything he couldn't deliver.

Louise took the packet and opened it. She spilled a pill into her hand.

"You take one a day," Gus told her. "Don't chew it. If you do, you have to swallow over and over again to get it down— otherwise it sticks in your throat. It might be better if you took it with some water."

"Maybe your grandmother should have these, since she's the one who's sick," Louise suggested.

"No, no. She's practically too sick for pills. Put anything in her and it comes right back up, even chicken broth," Gus insisted. He was finding that once he started lying, it got easier to just keep piling the lies on, one on top of another. It was not a good feeling.

"Well, I'll try them," Louise said. "But you come tell me right away when it's all right for me to come up again to see the ducks, okay?"

"Yep," Gus assured her. "But I don't think it'll be for a while. She's pretty sick."

With that final lie hanging in the air, Gus climbed on the bike and pedaled slowly across the scruffy grass to the road. He looked back once as he headed down the hill. Louise was standing at the end of the garden, one hand clutching the Vimms, and the other waving to him. He took one hand off the handlebars and offered a feeble wave in return. Right about then, he thought, with his hand raised as a target, would be a good time for that lightning bolt to appear out of the clear blue sky and strike him dead. Lord knew, he deserved it.

Chapter Eight

As soon as the ducks were released from the brooder, they became Gus's almost constant companions. When he went to the chicken coop in the morning to let them out, they gathered at his feet like expectant campers waiting to see what the day's activities would be. If Gus's grandmother went to the coop before he did to gather eggs, they would file out in a stately procession and settle down under one of the big maple trees in the front yard to wait for his highness to appear. If he was late in the afternoon sneaking them a tidbit from the kitchen, they collected just beyond the back steps and said unkind things about him. And within a week, he was chasing them out of the garden half a dozen times a day for waddling over and through his grandmother's precious vegetables.

In spite of their company, Gus was lonely. The worst of it was that he had brought it on himself. He moped through his chores and was impatient with the ducks. At times he even wished school would start so he might meet other boys his age. When he could, he would take one of his comic books outside to read in the shade of a maple tree. While he was lying immobile, the ducks took a perverse delight in pecking harmlessly at his toes, as though they were juicy worms presented for dessert. Gus missed Louise and her sense of humor, the way she would have laughed until her eyes teared the time he decided to wiggle his toes and make his feet jump. The ducks fell over themselves trying to escape and ended up in a noisy pile of loose, floating feathers. Louise would have enjoyed the way they lined up, their beady eyes bright with confidence in their leader. She and Gus would have led them on parades up and down the road, through the fields, wherever the world might be brightened by a little pomp and ceremony. But without Louise, Gus had neither the inclination nor the imagination to play with the ducks. They weren't toys, and as his grandpa had said, they weren't kittens. To Gus, they were just ducks. Precious and cute but not the same as a friend.

A week after Louise had been banned from the farm, Gus and his grandmother were standing in the Victory Garden considering the damage the ducks had wrought. His grandpa had come in after surveying the garden before breakfast and announced that it looked like Atlanta when Sherman laid waste to it in the Civil War.

"You'll have to keep them out of my garden, Gus," his grandmother said with her hands on her broad hips. She spoke without even trying to hide her exasperation. "Those ducks may be cute as dumplings, but they have no respect for my plants. They walk all over them. And excuse me for saying what no lady would ever mention, but they relieve themselves anywhere they have a mind to."

"Can we put up a fence?" Gus asked, trying to imagine how he was going to keep his ducklings away from their favorite feeding ground.

"Not with a war on," his grandmother said. "There's no wire for fencing and no money to buy it with. You'll have to do the best you can with whatever you can find around here. But remember, that garden is next winter's food. If the ducks ruin it, we'll all go hungry."

Suddenly, her eyes narrowed, and she looked sharply toward the road. Gus turned to look, too. "Who is that?" she asked.

"Louise! I think it's Louise!" Gus said, his face turning hot and his heart starting to race.

"Well, what do you suppose she's doing here?"

"I don't know." Gus swallowed hard. "I told her she couldn't come."

"I could have guessed that," his grandmother said. "You've been such a sad sack all week, I've been feeling sorry for you."

Gus and his grandmother strolled out to the road, followed by the ducks, and met Louise as she arrived, slightly winded, at the edge of the yard.

"How are you, Mrs. Amsler?" Louise asked.

"I'm perfectly fine, child," Gus's grandmother replied. Her arms were folded across her formidable chest, and Gus thought she looked like a fortress.

"I'm glad to hear that. Look what I brought you." Louise smiled warmly. She reached into her pocket and pulled out the package of Vimms. "Gus bought these for me last week because he thought I was sick, but I've been testing myself every day"—and with that she put the back of her hand to her forehead—"and I don't think I'm sick at all. But Gus said *you* were sick, so I decided you should have them. I've only taken one of them. They cost a lot of money, and the person who needs them should have them."

"Oh, I'm sick, am I?" Gus's grandmother asked, turning to Gus, whose face was redder than any sunburn could turn it.

Suddenly, Gus's grandfather was standing in the front doorway.

"Gus, get your overalls in here this instant!" he bellowed. "Your father's on the telephone, and he wants to talk to you. Don't make him stand there throwing his money away through the telephone wires. Nothing but an emergency would make him place a long-distance call, so get a move on, lad."

Gus forgot Louise and his grandmother and sprinted for the door. It must be about his mother, he thought. His heart was in his throat as he picked up the hearing piece and put his mouth to the speaker mounted on the big oak telephone.

"Dad? Dad? Is it really you?" He heard his father laugh, and all the tension was released as if a balloon had popped. "Is Mom okay?"

"Yep, Gus, it's really me, and your mother is coming along, no doubt due to all that fresh air and those weekly knock-knock jokes you send. That's not what this call is about. But, first, Buster, how are you? It's wonderful to hear your voice."

"I'm okay," Gus assured him. "Grandma and Grandpa are great. I've got three ducklings left, and they follow me everywhere. I wish you could see them."

"I wish I could see them, too," his father said, sounding sad and far away.

"What's wrong, Dad? Why are you calling?"

"I'm calling because you wrote to me and said you needed my help right away," his father explained.

"Oh, that. Dad, I'm in such a big hole," Gus lamented.

"It does sound like you dug yourself a beauty."

"But I was just trying to help," Gus protested. "It's not fair."

"What's not fair? You having a mother and a father, plus a grandmother and a grandfather, who keep you warm and fed and put a roof over your head while loving you like you're the only boy on the face of the earth and it's our mission to protect you from making mistakes? Sorry, Gus, everybody makes mistakes and everyone has to do his level best to fix them."

"But that's just it, Dad. I was only trying to help," Gus repeated.

"Lying and stealing hardly seem like the most direct route to doing good."

"What should I do?" Gus moaned.

"You already know what to do," his father pointed out. "I'm just calling to tell you I love you and miss you. Being apart is even harder than I thought it was going to be. I miss your mother so much, too."

"She *is* getting better, isn't she?"

"She's getting better even as we speak," his dad assured him. "Listen, I have class now, and I've got to run. No one is very keen around here about anyone being tardy. You give my love to Grandma and Grandpa, and thank them for taking such good care of you."

And then the line went dead. Gus lost his chance to tell his dad that he loved him. Almost as bad, his dad hadn't given him any advice on how to handle the situation he had put himself in. He just said that Gus knew what to do—and he supposed that he did, even if it meant that Louise never spoke to him again and his grandmother rightfully shipped him off to some other relative. His feet felt as heavy as potted plants as he walked to the front door.

Out in the yard, his grandmother and Louise stood side by side facing him, their arms folded across their chests and their expressions sour. The ducks stood by in a small huddle, like the seconds in duels who used to come along to make sure the fight was fair. Gus gulped. He crossed the yard until he stood directly in front of all of them.

"Grandma and Louise, I'm sorry," he mumbled, looking at the ground. Their expressions were too painful to face.

"Speak up, young man," his grandmother said. "You've got a lot to explain, and Louise and I want to make sure we don't miss one word of it."

"Grandma, I took the twenty-nine cents." Now the words came out in a tumble. "I took money from the egg jar because I didn't have enough bug money to buy Louise a package of Vimms. I thought I could pay you back before you noticed. Louise, I wanted to buy you the Vimms because I don't want you to get rickets like your father has. The government says that three out of four Americans are vitamin starved. Grandma, I let you think Louise stole the money because I was afraid you'd make me go live somewhere else if you knew I'd stolen the money. Louise, I told you Grandma was sick because I couldn't tell you that Grandma and Grandpa thought you were a thief and wouldn't let you come to the farm anymore. I am *so* sorry about everything. It just got out of control, and now everyone's mad at me, and I'll probably have to leave Miller's Run." Gus had tears in his eyes, but he refused to let them fall.

"I'm not mad at you, Gus. I'm disappointed," his grandmother said. "Oh, posh! I'm probably mad at you, too. But don't worry; we wouldn't send you away. You're not going anywhere until either your mother or father can take you home. But mark my words, you're going back to Boston a wiser young man than you came."

"Well, *I'm* mad at you," Louise said, her voice hard. "You let your grandparents think I'm a thief. I should drop these Vimms down the outhouse."

"Don't you do that, Louise," Gus's grandmother said. "Gus is probably right that it wouldn't hurt you to take a few vitamins. Might even put some pink in your cheeks. And besides, they cost good money, money that Gus worked hard to earn and my chickens did, too, by laying their eggs. I think we'll just have to find another way for Gus to work off his debt to *both* of us. You can start by coming up with a way to keep your ducks out of my garden. And Louise, I owe you an apology for thinking you were a thief. Old beliefs die hard."

And with that, she strode across the yard and slammed the front door behind her.

"Don't look at me," Louise warned as Gus turned to her. "They're not my ducks, and I didn't lie to anyone. I'm not so sure I want to have anything to do with you."

"Louise, I just didn't want you to get sick," Gus pleaded.

"Do I look sick?"

Gus snuck a glance at her, but he kept his mouth closed.

"Tell you what. Let's find out who's sickly. We'll arm-wrestle. I work like a horse at my house. I'll bet I'm stronger than you are. If I win, that'll prove I'm not sick, and then I'm going home and I'm not coming back. But if you win, then maybe you're right. I'll take the Vimms and help you find some way to keep the ducks out of the garden."

Gus considered Louise. She was scrawny, but he didn't doubt that every pound on her frame was muscle and grit. His life, in contrast, was pretty cushy. He hoped he could win. He took a deep breath and nodded to her.

They lay down in the grass in the front yard facing each other and angled themselves elbow to elbow. The ducks settled down nearby as if they'd paid admission to the show. Gus was surprised at the strength of Louise's grip. Then Louise shocked him by racing through the preamble in French. "*Un, deux, trois,* go!"

He wasn't ready, and Louise quickly bent his arm back halfway to the ground. He struggled, trying hard not to bend his wrist. Having lied to her, he had to win this fair and square. Louise had her tongue caught between her teeth and her eyes fastened on their hands. Slowly, Gus inched their fists toward center, past center, halfway down. Louise scooted her legs up under her until she was kneeling, so that she could throw her weight into her grip, but Gus kept pushing and Louise's hand moved inexorably toward the ground. By the time it touched, Gus had beads of sweat popping out on his forehead. Louise looked sad, as if she still wanted to march down the road and never come back.

Instead, she stood up and brushed off her overalls.

"A deal's a deal," she said, and, he didn't think it possible, but he felt even worse than before. Here was Louise, with nothing, showing herself to be a person of honor when only moments before he'd been apologizing for being both a liar and a thief.

"You just need to keep scaring them," Louise said matter-of-factly. "Look at them. They are—how do you say it—scaredy cats." She kicked her foot in their direction, and the ducks bolted from their ringside seats and made enough noise to herald the Second Coming.

That's how Gus and Louise happened to find themselves collecting a half can of assorted garden beetles and worms and scattering them in the front yard to occupy the ducks so they could sneak away. They headed out to the woods beyond the fields to collect sticks, anything a yard or so long and reasonably straight.

"Here, use the hammer I found in the barn," Gus said to Louise as they worked their way around the perimeter of the garden pounding in stakes. Then they went into the barn and rooted around in the pile of feedbags until they had half a dozen that could be torn into strips. They tied the strips to the tops of the stakes and stood back to watch the breeze play with the makeshift banners.

"That might do it," Gus's grandmother said as she came out to the back porch door and assessed the stakes, which stood like crooked sentinels with flags snapping from their heads. "It's worth a try."

Out front the ducks were raising an awful racket. Gus's grandfather had said they were better at guarding the place than a dog. Gus, Louise, and Gus's grandmother walked around to the front of the house.

The ducklings were on their tiptoes, flapping their wings in a cloud of loose feathers and quacking at a man who was standing in the road and catching his breath after having climbed the hill.

Gus thought the man was about his father's age, but his face had more lines, as if he'd spent a lot of time outside. Although they had obviously started out green and blue, his pants and shirt were about the same color of dusty brown after the climb up the dry road. On his back he carried a large, bulging rucksack.

"That's quite a welcoming committee you've got there," he said, smiling at the ducks.

"Mr. Thompson, how nice to see you. Oh, hush!" Gus's grandmother said, turning to flick her apron smartly at the ducks. The ducks responded to this new development by running around and making even more noise. "It must be a good three months since you've been here."

"About that," Mr. Thompson said. He looked around. "I hope no one's tried to horn in on my territory."

"Oh, mercy, no," Gus's grandmother replied. "I think Miller's Run is too hilly for most peddlers. It takes a pretty determined salesman to make his way to the top of this hill."

"I can't believe there's a man alive who wouldn't climb that hill if he knew he'd be greeted by your sunny face," Mr. Thompson said to Gus's grandmother. He winked at Gus and Louise.

"Your flattery will get you a glass of water," Gus's grandmother said, blushing and smiling. "Have a seat."

"Who are you two?" Mr. Thompson asked as he slipped off his rucksack and sat down on the big granite stoop.

"I'm August Amsler the third," Gus said. He got to use his full name so infrequently that when he did, he liked to make it sound as though it was two or three feet long.

Mr. Thompson looked Gus over from head to foot. "You've got some mighty big shoes to fill, young man. And who might this pretty young lady be?" He turned to Louise with her dirt-streaked face and black fingernails.

"Louise Lavictoire," Louise said. "I live over on Cherry Hill."

"I know very well where you live," Mr. Thompson said. "I suppose I know where everyone lives."

Gus's grandmother appeared in the doorway with a glass of water.

"Here I am gabbing away, when Mrs. Amsler and I have some important business to transact. If you'll excuse me . . ." Mr. Thompson untied the string on his rucksack and began pulling out lumpy rolls of cloth. He laid these on the stoop, untied more strings and unrolled them. Each was like a small store window with a theme: cooking, sewing, baking, tableware.

Gus was fascinated. No one came to their apartment in Boston and tried to sell his mother anything. His family always went to a store to buy what they needed. He took a step closer to get a better look at Mr. Thompson's wares.

"I know I need sewing needles," Gus's grandmother said. "They may be made of steel, and we're supposed to be saving steel for the war effort, but I don't know how they expect anyone to sew a stitch of clothing—not to mention mending the clothing we already have—if we don't have needles. I also need black, white, and blue thread."

"I think I can help you there," Mr. Thompson said, pulling out a packet of three needles and handing them up to Gus's grandmother for her inspection.

Twenty minutes later, Gus's grandmother had bought the needles and thread and a butter knife. "I'll also take a jelly spoon if I have enough credit. Mine is worn clear out. Let me get the rags," she said when she was done shopping.

She stepped back into the house and returned minutes later with an old pillowcase made from a bleached feedbag. It hung heavily at the bottom, as if it had a possum in it, and she handed it to Mr. Thompson. He reached in and started pulling out pieces of cloth, flowered scraps that Gus knew must once have been part of one of his grandmother's aprons or dresses, white scraps that he recognized as feed sacks made over into dishtowels, torn cheesecloth that he remembered seeing in the kitchen when his grandmother used it to drain the whey from the cottage cheese she made.

"I think you've got enough here for that jelly spoon, Mrs. Amsler." Mr. Thompson fully unrolled the display of tableware and selected for her a small tin spoon with a delicately scrolled handle.

Mr. Thompson returned Gus's grandmother's empty pillowcase to her and started packing the rags into the bottom of his pack. Then he rolled up his wares and put them back. Finally, he stood up. "As for you two," he said, turning to Gus and Louise, "here's a treat for having the good sense to associate with this fine woman." He reached into his pants pocket and drew out two peppermints.

Louise gasped.

"I think you should have some biscuits to take with you," Gus's grandmother said. She disappeared yet again and returned with an old napkin folded carefully around a handful of biscuits left over from dinner.

"I'm much obliged." Mr. Thompson doffed his hat and bowed to her. "As always, it's been a pleasure doing business with you, Mrs. Amsler. I'll make sure I stop by next time I'm passing through."

"You do that, Mr. Thompson. Until then, God bless you," Gus's grandmother said.

As soon as Mr. Thompson had disappeared over the brow of the hill, Louise said, "I have to go."

"Aren't you going to have your peppermint?" Gus asked. His was already melting in a pocket in his mouth and making the inside of his cheek numb.

"No. I'll take it home and share it," Louise said. She wrapped her dirty hand tightly around the candy.

"Can I take Louise on the bike, Grandma?" Gus asked.

"As long as your grandfather doesn't have anything for you to do," she said. She turned and disappeared into the house with her purchases, the pillowcase, and the empty water glass.

"Before you go," Gus said, "take a Vimms. You've already wasted a week."

"That's not my fault," Louise reminded him. She reached into her pocket and took out the package of pills. She removed a pill and sniffed it.

"Swallow it," Gus urged her, a little louder than he intended.

Louise put the pill on the tip of her tongue, and within seconds the corners of her mouth were turned down in a grimace.

"Swallow it!"

Louise swallowed and gagged, then tried again. Finally, the pill went down. She spat on the grass and put her hands to her throat.

"If that is what vitamins taste like, I think I'd rather get rickets," Louise said, still spitting on the grass.

"Maybe you should try it next time with water," Gus said.

Gus knew the pills wouldn't work right away. He didn't feel one degree more alive since he'd taken his Vimms, so he was now torn between skepticism and hopefulness.

But he didn't want to think that he had wasted his money and caused so much trouble for nothing. He couldn't help looking for changes when Louise climbed off the handlebars back at her house. When she turned around to say goodbye, he asked, "Do you feel stronger yet?"

"No," Louise said. "I feel the same."

"I think your cheeks are pinker," Gus said, studying her.

"They are?" Louise raised a hand to her cheek and left a new smudge of dirt beneath her eye.

"Well, let me know if you feel any different," Gus told her. "You have twenty-two pills left."

That night after supper, while Gus was drying the dishes his grandmother handed to him, he asked, "What does Mr. Thompson do with the rags?"

"He sells them to a papermaker, who uses them to make paper," his grandmother said. "Are you just curious? Seems to me there's a point to your question."

"I was just wondering," Gus said. "While I was taking Louise home, she asked if we had lots of rags."

"Why would she ask a question like that?" Gus's grandmother said, turning toward him. She paused with her hands deep in the sink while soapy water ran down her forearms.

"She said, if we did, if we had extras, maybe her mama could use them to sew dresses and shirts for her little brothers and sisters," Gus said.

"Good gracious!" Gus's grandmother said. "They're nothing but a snippet of this, a scrap of that. They're rags. They're hardly fit for a dog to sleep on."

"That's what I thought," Gus said.

Chapter Nine

By the middle of August, Vermont was so ripe it hurt Gus's eyes to look at all that bright green. Every week or so his grandfather climbed on his tractor to keep the fields from growing up to puckerbrush, and so he could share hay with anyone in Miller's Run who was running short.

His grandmother's Victory Garden was justly named. As far as Gus could tell, it had won the war against bugs, the ducks, and Vermont's fickle weather and was growing out of control. Gus spent every morning in the garden snapping beans from their stems while the ducks squatted unhappily in the grass, nervously eyeing the fluttering strips of cloth that he and Louise had posted. Thanks to the ducks' and his own attentive picking of potato bugs, the potatoes had blossomed into small bushes. He had to take his grandmother's word that underneath the soil was a winter's worth of mashed potatoes, but the bushy parts looked almost fit enough to eat as well. Onion tops lined up neatly in long rows like soldiers awaiting orders from their commanders. He liked having onions again to mix with the gravy his grandmother poured over the potted meat to make it taste better. Sometimes he thought that if potted meat was all he was going to get for the duration of the war, he'd just as soon that the United States surrender right now, but he knew better than to complain. Besides, every night when he carried slops to the pig, he looked at that enormous sow and could almost taste the bacon she would provide. With her piglets gone to other farmers, she had nothing to do, Gus figured, except stare at him malevolently with her beady eyes and eat until she could feed the three of them for a whole year.

"Looks like you've got yourself some mallards. They are surely beautiful," Gus's grandfather said to Gus and Louise the afternoon they got ready to round up the ducks to take them down to the pond to release them.

And they were. The two larger ducks, Roosevelt and Louis, had turned out to be males. As their feathers had grown in, the drakes had developed iridescent green heads that caught the light and made them glow like stained glass windows. Both of them had a thin ribbon of white around their throats, like a collar. Their bodies were covered in richly colored feathers of brown and blue and gray, and their white tail feathers flanked a couple of dark feathers that turned up in a stylish bob at the end. Candy, the only female, was still a runt. She wore a drab dress of browns, from tawny to mud to beige, all designed to camouflage her in the bulrushes, where, Gus hoped, she would one day keep her nest with babies of her own. Plain and simple like her coloring was a fringe of white around her tail, which stuck out straight behind her like a flag caught in a stiff breeze.

The roundup began calmly. Gus walked to the edge of grass fronting the road and waited for the ducks to line up behind him, which they obediently did. Louise stepped in front of Gus and raised her fist. In it she held one of the sticks from the garden, with a strip of feedbag still tied to it and flitting gently in the afternoon air. When the parade was organized, Louise stepped out smartly and marched across the road and into the stubble on the opposite side. The ducks followed Gus as far as the cut hay and stopped. Their heads bobbed up and down as they tried to keep an eye on him, but they refused to step into grass that was half as tall as they were.

"Hey, ducks," Gus called softly.

They stood their ground. He called again. The ducks began to engage in a noisy debate of the perils toward which Gus was luring them. Despite the faith they had shown all their lives in their leader, they refused to budge. They had reached the outer boundaries of their universe and would not step off the edge.

After fifteen fruitless minutes, Gus, Louise, and Gus's grandfather returned to the barn. They came out carrying feed sacks, and proceeded to chase the ducks around the road in front of the barn. The ducks gabbled testily. Poorly designed for land travel, they waddled awkwardly in big circles, bobbing from side to side on their big orange feet like heavyweight fighters and flapping their full-grown wings. The air quickly filled with small feathers.

"Catch Candy, Grandpa!" Gus yelled to his grandfather as he lunged after one of the drakes. Gus caught it by the neck and shoved it rudely into the sack head-first. Inside, it quacked as if it wanted to share this indignity with the whole town of Miller's Run. At the same time, Candy darted between his grandfather's legs and gave him a good crack on both shins with her wings. He grunted and did a quick two-step, but instead of catching her, he landed on his backside in the road. Fine dust blew up in a cloud mingled with feathers. Louise made the mistake of starting to laugh. Gus looked at his grandfather sitting unceremoniously in the middle of the road, his hat askew, and he started laughing, too. Gus's grandmother came out on the front stoop to see what all the commotion was about.

"You three are certainly making quite a flap," she observed above the mayhem.

"Flap. Get it?" Gus gasped between spasms of laughter.

Louise and Gus starting running in circles, flapping their arms like wings.

Gus's grandfather removed his hat and began swatting at the dust and feathers. This, of course, only made the two remaining ducks more skittish. The loose drake decided he'd had enough and took off down the road, his wings fully extended and his voice in fine form. Candy had retreated to the yard and was surveying the chaos as if she were the only sane person in the asylum.

"Well, go get him!" Louise sputtered. Gus handed his roiling bag to his grandfather and ran after the escapee. Louise turned her attention to Candy, who pirouetted on her defective orange foot while Louise circled her, holding a feed-bag. After several minutes of circling and getting nothing, Louise launched herself through the air and tackled Candy, but Candy fought back, yanking Louise's hair out in small tufts with her bill. Gus, coming back up the road with the renegade drake kicking and quacking in a feedbag, convulsed in laughter and collapsed.

When the Battle of the Ducks finally ended, the victors were a sorry lot. All three were on the ground. Gus's grandfather was still swatting the air with his hat in one hand while he held a wriggling feedbag in the other. Louise had one hand on her squirming bag, and with the other hand she was feeling tenderly about her scalp, investigating her new bald spots. Gus's dirty face was streaked from tears of laughter. Small downy feathers adhered to the wet streaks, creating a striped effect—half werewolf, half boy. Together, all three gave the impression that the devil itself had just been rousted from the Amsler Farm.

"Give me a hand up, Gus," his grandfather asked. "I haven't been in this position since I learned how to stay out of the way of a cow's tail forty years ago."

"Not a one of you is allowed in my house," Gus's grandmother announced from the stoop, and then she went inside.

But the ducks had been caught. Gus, his grandfather, and Louise carried the sacks down to the edge of the pond while the captives struggled furiously. Gus was sure that once the ducks were released they would be astonished by the sight of so much water and would rush into the pond, but that didn't happen. Gus let one drake out first, and it immediately turned around and started waddling quickly back up the hill toward the barn. He let the second one go, and it did the same thing. When Candy was released, she just followed the others.

Shocked and embarrassed by what he considered their unducklike behavior, Gus caught up to them and managed to turn them around and herd them back toward the pond. He worked them right up to the edge by flapping his arms and ignoring his grandfather's chuckles and Louise's big grin. Once he had them on the bank, he waited for them to dive in, as he thought any self-respecting duck would. Instead, they gabbled nervously on the bank and refused to budge. Finally, Gus grabbed one of the males under its soft wings and threw it onto the water, surprised, as he always was when he handled the ducks, at how nearly weightless they were. It landed on its brown stomach with a splash and started swimming. Encouraged, he gently swept up Candy and threw her in, too. Taking the hint, the last duck dove in behind the others, and all three of them swam to the safety of the middle of the pond and treaded water, gossiping among themselves about the afternoon's events.

"Why didn't they just jump in, Grandpa?" Gus asked while they stood there watching. All his life he'd heard the expression "like a duck takes to water," but here he couldn't for the life of him coax his ducks into the pond. In fact, he'd had to throw them like bales of hay. It wasn't the first time he'd been perplexed by the ducks' behavior, but if they thought that, as their mother, he was supposed to jump into the pond first, well, they had another think coming.

"They're confused, Gus," his grandfather said. "They're wild ducks, but they've always lived in a barnyard with a bowl of water you've put down in front of them. Give them some time. They'll get used to it." Then he headed up to the barn to wash up.

Gus and Louise stayed to watch the ducks. Reluctant as they had been to get in the water, they certainly didn't need any swimming lessons. They floated like corks and paddled gracefully around. They swatted their open wings against the water's surface and kicked up small showers and smaller waves, and seemed to enjoy dipping their heads quickly in and out of the water and letting the droplets stream off their feathers like strings of pearls.

Walking back up to the barn to do their own cleaning up, Gus took the opportunity to study Louise out of the corner of his eye. He thought she was definitely looking more vigorous and alive now that she'd been taking Vimms vitamins for close to two weeks. Almost as soon as she started taking them, they'd decided to split the pills in half to make them last as long as possible. Gus figured that if she ultimately took the full dose, she'd get the full effect. He had also persuaded his grandmother not only to let Louise back in the kitchen but also to offer her a glass of Ovaltine almost every time she visited. Gus didn't like the chalky chocolate taste himself, but he drank his, too, just to be companionable. The best part was that Louise didn't even know she was getting something that was supposed to make her sparkle.

Sunlight shot through the canopy of the trees overhead and mottled the grass around them as they walked toward the barn to clean themselves up. As they washed their hands and arms in a bucket of water, Gus gathered his courage and spoke up. "Grandma says it's okay if you want to come to the fair."

Louise's eyes lit up. "The fair?" she asked, as if Gus had invited her to go to the moon.

"The county fair," Gus said. "It's next week."

"With the war, I didn't know if they'd have the fair," Louise said.

"It's small," Gus said, just repeating what his grandmother had told him. He had never been to a fair, so he didn't have any idea what "small" meant. Still, it sounded exciting to him. At least, it was something different from the quiet routine of the farm. "Grandpa says there won't be any fireworks. The army needs the explosives, and anyway, fireworks have to be put off at night, when the Germans might see them and bomb us."

Louise's eyes grew even bigger. "Why would they bomb *us?*"

"Vermont helps make ships and tanks and planes to send overseas," Gus explained, proud to know something that Louise didn't. "If the Germans get this far, Vermont would be one of its targets." He spoke with authority even though he and his grandfather had yet to see any evidence of a German plane. Gus didn't even know what a German looked like, except dead, from *Life* magazine. He had studied photographs of the corpses of German soldiers, trying to discover what set them apart, what made them so bad that his dad was willing to leave him and his mother to go fight them. So far he hadn't found anything to distinguish them. He thought they looked a lot like most of the people he had seen on the sidewalks of Boston. Come to think of it, Louise and her family with their dark hair and gaunt bodies looked more different to him than the Germans did.

"It's Monday, Tuesday, and Wednesday, next week, in Tunbridge," Gus told her. "We're going on Tuesday, because that's the day they judge the vegetables. Grandpa says Grandma always takes her vegetables and her canning to compete against the produce of every other woman in the county. It's sort of a tradition. There may be a war going on, but he says she's not going to stop trying to outdo all the other ladies in the county for anything short of the end of the world."

Louise sat quietly.

"Your mother has a garden," Gus said after a while. "Is she going to take anything?"

"I've heard about the fair, but we have never gone," Louise said quietly. "But I would like to go. I will ask Mama and Papa."

That night in bed, Gus listened for the ducks. He had gone down to the pond after supper with one of his grandmother's rolls. The ducks were quietly gathered together in the middle of the water, like a flotilla at anchor.

"Hey, ducks," he had called and started tossing bits of bread onto the water.

They swam over as one and grabbed at the sodden bread until the roll was gone. When Gus showed them his empty hands, they paddled away.

Now, as he lay in bed listening for any sounds that might indicate they were in trouble, Gus felt as if some part of him were missing—nothing quite as big as an arm or a leg, but something that was nevertheless essential. He had never *owned* the ducks. He knew that. But they were a part of him, and now he knew from watching them on the pond that some threshold had been crossed. They didn't need him anymore. Even if they never saw him again, they would probably survive. In just two months they had grown independent, while he, at thirteen years old, could hardly imagine being so alone and free. He didn't even want to consider it. Instead, he closed his eyes and prayed as he did every night that he, his mother, and his father would be reunited soon.

Chapter Ten

The next Tuesday, everyone was up early. The day dawned heavy with bright gray clouds that made Gus squint despite the lack of sun. His grandmother bustled around with the energy of three people until a thin film of sweat shone on her face. Her tight bun loosened from her exertions, and white hair began to curl around her red face like fringe. Gus and his grandfather just took orders. They brought the picnic hamper up from the cellar for her, and she filled it with deviled eggs, cold sliced potted meat, potato salad, lemonade, and slices of last night's blueberry pie.

Gus's grandmother made numerous trips to the cellar to bring up jars of vegetables that she'd been canning for the past week: dilly green beans, pickled beets, carrots, and corn relish. She stood on the stoop of the back porch and held each jar up to the light.

"What are you looking for, Grandma?" Gus asked. He was standing behind her and trying to see whatever she was studying.

"A glow," she said firmly. "The judges want to see something so fresh it's practically growing out of the jar."

Nothing in the jars looked to Gus as if it would be growing much more, but he held his tongue. He kept quiet later, too, when his grandmother went out to her Victory Garden to choose this year's prize-winning vegetables. He knew that his own work as the garden's caretaker would now be put to the ultimate test. Fortunately, she came in carrying a basket heavily laden with tomatoes and beans and cabbage. She carefully washed the produce in the sink and then watched it drip while she snapped her head from side to side searching for imperfections, particularly any damage wrought by worms that Gus and the ducks had failed to catch and destroy.

"I guess all my good dishtowels are upstairs on the guest bed. Would you please fetch me half a dozen, Gus?" his grandmother asked.

Gus climbed the stairs to the guest room, where the towels were laid out fresh and crisp from ironing. As he grabbed them, marveling as he always did that his grandmother ironed the towels she dried her vegetables in, he saw draped across the foot of his aunt's childhood bed the quilt his grandmother had finished several evenings earlier. Downstairs, Gus handed the towels to his grandmother.

"Why don't you take your new quilt, Grandma?" he asked.

"Because Karen Kitzmiller is a good woman and one of my closest friends, and she can sew a stitch so fine you'd almost go blind trying to find it," his grandmother replied. "I have no intention of exposing my handiwork to public scrutiny within five miles of anyplace her quilts are on display."

When she was done wrapping the vegetables in damp dishtowels to keep them fresh, she and his grandfather, who had been layering hay in the back of the truck, went upstairs to dress.

"Put on something with no holes," she instructed Gus over her shoulder. "And wear a clean shirt."

While Gus was upstairs, he jotted his weekly note to his mother so they could drop it at the post office as they went through town.

> *Dear Mom,*
> *Knock-knock.*
> *Who's there?*
> *Porpoise.*
> *Porpoise who?*
> *Porpoise of this note is to tell you we're going to the fair today! Louise is going, too.*
>
> > *Love,*
> > *Your son, Gus*

His mother really got a kick out of his knock-knock jokes. Gus could tell, because she had started sending her own each week to him now. Her last one had read,

> *Knock-knock.*
> *Who's there?*
> *Mission.*
> *Mission who?*
> *Mission you a lot!*

It was one more note preserved in the loft in the barn, where he could burrow down in the hay on rainy days with the summer's mail and almost pretend his family was together again. His dad always wrote about what he was learning. He was soloing now and practicing snap rolls and slow rolls. He said he could fly so high he could practically see Vermont from Texas. Gus couldn't imagine seeing the world all laid out before you like a gigantic tablecloth, the thin roads a tangle of brown ribbons, the fields and forests scattered like dropped napkins, and the people on the ground so insignificant that they were invisible.

He was surprised half an hour later when his grandparents came down in their Sunday clothes. His grandmother wore her best dress, the navy one with a white lace collar crocheted like a doily, and her best blue shoes. But no stockings. He'd heard that lots of women had turned in their silk stockings for salvage. Silk was hard to come by during the war when the Army Air Forces needed all the silk they could lay their hands on to make parachutes for the men overseas. Gus's grandfather was wearing his black suit, shiny with age and wear but still serviceable, as his grandmother would say. In place of his usual hat, he carried a dark gray fedora with a black grosgrain ribbon around its crown.

Gus and his grandfather packed the jars into wood crates in the back of the truck, carefully cradling each jar in hay so it wouldn't break. Then his grandparents climbed into the cab, and Gus lifted himself over the tailgate into the back. The ride to Louise's was bouncy on the pitted road, but the humid air kept some of the dust down.

As the Lavictoires' littered yard came into view, Gus heard his grandmother exclaim, "For the love of heaven!"

Louise and her mother were waiting out front. As the truck slowed down, Gus's grandfather leaned out the window and spoke as softly to Gus as he could over the rattle of the wheels on the gravel.

"Be a gentleman. Make sure you get out and help her in."

Gus hopped out when the truck stopped, but Louise didn't need any help. She wasn't a delicate female, as his grandmother would say. She stepped up on the bumper and swung herself into the back.

Mrs. Lavictoire took a few hesitant steps toward Gus's grandmother's window. Her face was thin and drawn, and her faded green dress hung on her frame as if she were a skeleton, with one exception. Her stomach bulged where the baby was growing underneath it.

"Thank you. *Merci,*" she said softly and nodded. She kept her eyes cast down and smiled a smile so thin and small that it looked like a paper cut on her face.

"It's our pleasure, Mrs. Lavictoire. Louise is a delightful child," Gus's grandmother said, leaning out the window and raising her voice nearly to a shout, apparently believing that the volume might somehow aid in the translation. "We'll be home late, but we'll make sure she gets something to eat."

Mrs. Lavictoire's head kept nodding, like an apple bobbing in a barrel of water. It was clear to Gus that she did not understand a single word his grandmother was saying, at this or any other volume.

In the bed of the truck, looking at Louise, Gus was sorry

there wasn't room for her up front in the cab. She had had a bath, not just a slapdash wash but a real scrubbing, probably even with soap. Her hair shone and her face was clean. For the first time, he noticed that her face was spangled with pale freckles, just like his. Louise, Gus was proud to say, positively sparkled. She was as buoyant as a person could be and still have her feet on the ground. Most surprising of all, she wore a dress. It was so faded that its print of small blue flowers was almost worn away. Here and there, it was held together with neat patches, but something about the dress seemed familiar to Gus. Then it came to him and he glanced over at the scarecrow, which stood nude amid the wild garden, its body and arms nothing but bare sticks beneath its straw-stuffed head. Somewhere, Louise had even found shoes. He estimated the brown oxfords were a size or two too big, and the soles were nearly worn through, but he was impressed. He could not imagine where the Lavictoires had found them. Louise looked at Gus and grinned, and then they started bouncing down the hill.

The fair was bustling. Gus's grandfather pulled the truck right up to the produce tent, and Gus and Louise helped unload his grandmother's vegetables onto the tables next to produce belonging to other ladies with equally high hopes. Gus's grandmother did not help. Instead, she stood regally by, as if she were a queen holding court, but Gus noticed that her eyes roamed nervously over the tables nearby, also laden with vegetables.

"We'll meet here at noon sharp for dinner," she said to

them as they finished unloading and she moved in to begin arranging. "And then you'll be free again until five o'clock."

"Here's fifty cents for each of you," Gus's grandfather said, pulling four shiny quarters from his pocket and dropping two each into Louise's and Gus's open hands. They looked at each other with bright eyes and laughed out loud.

If this was a small fair, Gus wondered, what had the big fairs before the war looked like? He and Louise wandered away from the vegetable tent to the tents where they could hear the bleating and honks of animals. Gus went over first to see the cows, not just the sweet brown cows like the ones his grandfather had kept, but the new black-and-white cows, the kind the younger farmers were trying out because they produced more milk. He and Louise admired the ducks, too. Some were white with orange feet and bills, but others were mallards, and they looked just like his drakes, their heads a luminous green that changed color in every light, or like Candy, with their browns soft and muted.

They spent more than an hour at the antiques exhibit. Some folks who, Gus thought, already looked as though they had been around to vote for Abraham Lincoln were dressed up in old-timey clothes. They wandered around demonstrating how *their* grandparents had churned butter and scythed their fields by hand. Gus couldn't even identify half the tools and contraptions.

"I don't see why they think this stuff is old," Louise sniffed while they were watching the scything demonstration. "My papa cuts the fields that way."

"Why don't you get a tractor?" Gus asked, and then felt

his face flush. Many of the farmers in Miller's Run still didn't have tractors. Even if the Lavictoires were among those waiting for these newfangled mechanical labor-savers, they probably would be the last to scrape together enough money to buy one.

Louise ignored him and looked at a woman washing clothes. "And my mama uses one of those big tubs and a washboard every Monday."

This time Gus kept silent. He thought of his grandmother's Maytag washing machine tucked in a corner on the back porch. Sparkling white and big as a calf, with a roller that took the wettest tablecloth and reduced it to a nearly dry, flat pancake, it was one of the possessions she was proudest of.

Later on, they wandered over to the sideshows—the hairiest woman in the universe; Siamese twins, joined at the hip; the man who could whistle with his mouth full of water; the prettiest woman in the world.

"Over here! Over here!" the barkers cried, trying to lure people into the mysterious, beckoning tents. Gus's eyes were wide with wonder, but Louise was skeptical.

"If she's all that beautiful, why isn't she married and home, and if the hairy woman is all that ugly, seems like she'd want to stay home, too."

Taking their time, Gus and Louise lingered on the edge of the crowd enjoying the spectacle and listening to the people as they emerged from the various tents.

"That wasn't anything but a fat lady with a mustache glued on."

"If those twins were joined at the hip by anything other

than twine, I'll eat my cigar," one man complained as he struck a match and lit the end of his stogie.

Gus and Louise might have missed dinner entirely if someone walking by hadn't said, "Is it twelve o'clock already?" They raced back to the vegetable tent and found Gus's grandparents consulting with each other.

"Her beans are *not* nicer than mine," Gus's grandmother huffed. She folded her arms, grabbed her elbows, and scowled, her big chest rising and falling in indignation and hurt. "I have looked and looked, and I can't see one iota of difference between hers and mine."

"There, there, Lily," Gus's grandfather said consolingly. He patted her on the shoulder. "You took blue ribbons in everything else. Be generous, share the glory."

Lunch under some trees at the edge of the fairground was subdued, even though Louise and Gus were bursting with excitement from the morning's activities. When Gus's grandmother pulled out a plate of potted meat, Louise froze in the sharp, conspicuous way that a dog freezes when a cat catches its attention. Gus's grandmother paused briefly and then offered Louise a slice. They all watched as she took it and devoured it.

"I'm sorry," she said, when she noticed the attention she had drawn. She wiped at her chin with her plaid napkin. "I haven't eaten any meat but the squirrels my papa shot in a long time." When she was offered a second slice, and later a third, the others pretended not to notice how eagerly she ate every last morsel. After the picnic had been cleaned up and the hamper returned to the truck, Gus's grandfather invited

Gus and Louise to join him at the track to watch the racing.

"Don't corrupt them, August," Gus's grandmother warned, her good humor restored by the meal. "I'm headed for the crafts tent to see who has been crocheting and quilting over the winter."

Gus had never seen racehorses before. Sleek and fast, they glistened with sweat as they pounded their way down the track pulling the delicate sulkies. Behind them the jockies rode low, like chariot drivers. Over the clamor of hammering hooves, Gus's grandfather carried on loud conversations with other men about the merits of this horse or that. The folks crowded into the grandstand yelled and laughed as if they were at a big party. Great clouds of dust rose into the air and choked everyone. Eventually, the noise and dust grew to be too much. Gus and Louise could tell from the angle of the sun that the afternoon was waning. They left Gus's grandfather to the last few races and headed over to the rides.

They each still had their fifty cents to spend, and now they set about planning their entertainment. They rode first on the merry-go-round for a nickel apiece, but they agreed this was too tame. Gus chose the whirling swings next and almost lost his dinner. They both rode the Ferris wheel. As they reached the top of each revolution, they could see across the fairgrounds to the oxen-pulling contest. They tried to spot Gus's grandfather, but too many men were wearing black suits like his.

Then they moved on to the games of skill. Louise wasted one nickel trying to throw beanbags through holes in the painted face of a big clown, but the second time she managed to put a bag through an eye and a second bag through the clown's red nose. For her efforts, the carnival man gave her five pounds of sugar. Louise raised the bag over her head and danced. With the war on and sugar in short supply, her eyes glowed at the prize she could take home to her mother. Gus paid another nickel and tried his hand throwing darts at funny faces painted on the wall at the back of the booth. Target practice all summer with his grandfather's rifles must have refined his eye because all five of his darts found their target. None too happy, the barker handed Gus a stuffed blue rabbit that was almost two feet tall. Granted, it wasn't soft and furry like a rabbit—like so many items these days, from washcloths to shirts, it was made of dyed feedbags, with button eyes and nose—but Gus felt triumphant carrying his trophy through the fairgrounds. Their money finally gone, they saw it was time to drag themselves back to the truck.

Gus's grandmother was in fine humor now after winning a blue ribbon for her dilly beans, after which the judges ate every last one. She broke open another jar and gave them to Gus and Louise to share in the back of the truck on the way home. The rabbit and the bag of sugar rode up front with Gus's grandmother's precious blue ribbons.

"You take the rabbit," Gus insisted as he and Louise bounced along in the back of the truck.

"But you won it," Louise protested.

"I have my ducks," Gus countered. "And besides, your little brothers and sisters would like it."

"Thank you, *merci,* thank you," Louise babbled when Gus's grandfather stopped in front of the Lavictoires' to let her out.

Gus's grandmother smiled. "We were happy to have you, child," she said. She handed Louise her bag of sugar and then, when Gus insisted, the rabbit. "You're welcome any-time at the farm."

At home, though, Gus's grandmother had something else to say.

"How does anyone live like that?" she asked no one in particular as she unpinned her hat and hung it on the rack in the hall.

Dusk was falling, and Gus went down to the pond.

"Hey, ducks," he called and waited. The ducks were half wild now. They often passed the hottest part of the day hid-den in the bulrushes and cattails that rimmed the pond. At other times, they dabbled in the shallow water, grubbing for grasses. Whenever Gus went down to the pond to visit them, he was struck by how comfortable they were in their new home. It was hard to believe that just a few weeks ago they had followed him everywhere, pecking at his toes.

"Hey, ducks," he called again and waited. He had learned to be patient. Even if the ducks were hiding, they eventually came when he called because he always brought food. Some-times it was a crust of bread, sometimes a soggy shredded-wheat biscuit left over from breakfast. The ducks didn't seem particular; they were always eager for a treat.

This time only two ducks swam out from their nighttime roosts. Candy and one of the drakes, probably Roosevelt, paddled over and waited just out of reach while he broke a few crackers and scattered the crumbs on the water. The ducks attacked the crumbs fiercely, pushing and shoving, dipping their bills to mix the food with water. He threw some crumbs nearer Candy so she stood a better chance of reaching them first.

"Hey, ducks," he called again and waited.

His grandfather appeared behind him, still wearing his suit, even though the grass was wet with dew and sure to leave his pants legs damp.

"Where's the other drake?" his grandfather asked.

"I don't know," Gus said, beginning to worry. Cowards that they were, the ducks always acted together. If one came, they all came.

"Hey, ducks, hey, ducks," he called, louder and more urgently. Candy and Roosevelt slowly paddled in circles in front of him, awaiting anything else he might throw.

Five minutes passed.

"Must be something got it," Gus's grandfather remarked quietly.

"But what would get it?" Gus asked in agony.

"There aren't many animals I can think of that hunt during the day," his grandfather said. "Wouldn't have been a cat or a dog. The ducks are safe on the water. Could have been a snapping turtle, but these aren't ducklings anymore. They'd be a handful to pull under. My guess, it was a hunter. There are an awful lot of families barely getting enough to eat these days."

Chapter Eleven

School was scheduled to start two days after Labor Day. The latest letter from his dad had laid out the plans. He would continue his training in Lubbock, Texas, and Gus's mother would continue to lie in the sun like a drowsy turtle, breathing in the clean Adirondack air. Gus would have to ride the bike down the hill, toward the village, to one of Miller's Run's two white schoolhouses. Both accommodated all twelve grades in two rooms. The schoolhouse Gus would attend was just two miles away, an easy distance to cover for a strapping young boy with two healthy legs, his grandmother said. She saw no reason to waste any precious, rationed gas taking Gus to and from school in the truck.

Gus accepted the news that he wouldn't be going back to Boston yet—had even anticipated it—but it was hard to keep postponing his hopes. For the first time he sent his mother a letter that wasn't supposed to make her laugh.

> *Knock-knock.*
> *Who's there?*
> *Myth.*

Myth who?
Myth you.

"What's the teacher like?" Gus asked as he pedaled up the hill in front of the Lavictoires'. After two and a half months of climbing this hill, he could breeze to the top, even with Louise balanced on the handlebars. As they coasted to a stop, Louise's little brothers and sisters swarmed toward them like ants descending on a picnic.

"I don't know your teacher," Louise said as she climbed down off the handlebars.

"Aren't we in the same grade?" Gus asked, puzzled. They were both thirteen. He knew that because he'd broken down one day and asked her.

"Oui," she said. "I should be. But it's a small school. There are only two classrooms, same as in the one on the other side of the village. You'll be in sixth grade with Mrs. Brewster and all the upper graders, and I will be in fourth grade with Miss Pearson and all the little children." She waved her hand at her brothers and sisters, some of whom Gus knew were too little to attend any school.

"Why?" he asked.

"Because when I came here, I didn't know any English. Because I couldn't speak, they thought I must be stupid." Gus could see Louise's eyes sparking in anger from the indignity of being labeled before she could show them what she was made of.

"But you speak English just as good as I do," Gus protested.

"Sometimes better," Louise said, smiling.

"And you're not stupid," continued Gus, who had developed a keen appreciation of Louise's intelligence.

"No, but that didn't stop the teachers from thinking I am," Louise said. "My family's different from everyone else's in Miller's Run. We are Catholic and French, and life has been very hard for us here. We can't get any credit at the store. Papa can't get anyone to help him on the farm. Everyone is watching to see us fail, and so we probably will. Papa says we are almost out of money, but I once heard someone at the store say that even the poor farm is too good for the likes of us."

"Why did you come here if everything was going to be so hard?" Gus asked.

"My papa is the sixth of seven brothers," Louise explained. "His papa had no land left to give him, and Papa knows nothing but farming. He heard there was land here. And there was land." Louise laughed ruefully. "But there wasn't any hope."

The first day of school, Gus was put not in the sixth grade but in the seventh, because he had already learned so much of the material in school in Boston. He felt small sitting in that single room among several big boys, some of whom were in the twelfth grade and could go off to join the army in a month or two when they turned eighteen. Most boys in Miller's Run weren't even bothering to attend school. With help scarce and many of their fathers and older brothers enlisted, boys Gus's age were needed at home on the farm. Gus looked around and couldn't pick out a single potential friend from among this ragtag bunch.

Louise, on the other hand, was a giant among pygmies in the classroom for the lower grades. At recess, when Miss Pearson planted herself between the older and younger children so they couldn't mingle and get into trouble, he glanced across and saw Louise standing miserably in the middle of a circle of little girls who were singing and dancing around her as if she were a Maypole. He thought she looked about as unhappy as a wet cat.

~~~

Once school started, Gus usually saw Louise only at school for brief moments before classes started and after the last bell. When school ended, she hurried home with her younger brothers gamboling around her knees like lambs. She explained to Gus that her mother's baby was due any day, and her mother was too tired to do more than drag herself around the house.

Gus scurried to keep up with her until they reached where the road to Cherry Hill branched off from the road to Gus's grandparents' farm. He tried to get her to linger, and she made an effort to smile while she shook her head. Her mama needed her.

At school, Gus watched the young children playing tag around Louise as if she were made of granite and not flesh and blood. With her stringy hair and wan face, she wasn't looking very buoyant these days, he thought. The Vimms had run out, and whatever charm they may have provided had run out, too. The times Louise had climbed the hill to

Gus's house to check in on the ducks, he made sure to take her into the kitchen, but he knew that even two or three glasses of Ovaltine at one sitting wouldn't be enough to make her glimmer, let alone sparkle.

To Gus's surprise, shortly after school began, it recessed for two weeks. The war had taken so many young men from the town that every person—adult and child—old enough to pitch hay or dig potatoes was needed to get in the crops.

One night at dinner, Gus's grandfather was quieter than usual. Like Gus, he worked his way slowly through a plate of beets and potted meat with horseradish from the Victory Garden. The horseradish gave the bland meat some kick, but Gus found it hard to eat without curling up his nose. He had eaten worse, but he couldn't recall when. He hoped his grandmother wouldn't notice that he was mostly just moving things around on his plate. If she gave him her speech about how the men overseas would be happy to have a home-cooked meal if he didn't want it, he was tempted to offer to trade tonight's meal for whatever the soldiers had in their K-rations.

"Gus, it's time for you to pay your dues for lying and stealing a while back," his grandfather said when supper was almost over. He pushed his chair away from the table and put his big hands on his knees. "Since I have the equipment and the gas ration, and you have a pair of strong hands with nothing much to occupy them during this school recess, and Mr. Lavictoire has many hands—most of them not useful—and several big hayfields ready for a second cutting, I'm taking you over to the Lavictoires' in the morning with my tractor, and you are going to offer to hay his fields."

"Me?" Gus asked, astonished. "I don't know anything about haying a field."

"I guarantee you will before you're through," his grandfather said. "Get a good night's sleep. Tomorrow's going to be a long day."

The next morning, under a bright blue sky that promised to be perfect for haying, Gus helped his grandfather attach the cutter bar behind the tractor, then he climbed on the back and planted his feet on a crossbar behind the seat.

"Now, you hold on," his grandfather warned. "Your grandmother and your parents would never forgive me if you fell off the tractor and I ran over you. Killing the duck is all my old heart can take this season."

He put the tractor in gear and drove slowly down the road, spewing black smoke in front and kicking up dust behind. Two miles was a long ride, and Gus was nearly deaf when they arrived. While they were moving, he didn't dare take his hands off his grandfather's shoulders, but as soon as they stopped, he put two fingers in his mouth to make sure none of his teeth had rattled loose.

Mr. Lavictoire was up in the field behind the house scything. It was clear even to Gus that he moved with the grace of a dancer, lifting the scythe behind him and swinging it forward into the standing hay as if he were sluicing through running water itself. Mr. Lavictoire looked up once when the tractor appeared and then put down his scythe as it stopped in front of his house. He walked slowly through the field, stepped over the broken rail fence, and approached the tractor.

"We came to see if we could help you get your hay in," Gus's grandfather said.

Mr. Lavictoire shook his head. It wasn't a "no"; it looked to Gus more like confusion.

"Where's Louise?" Gus asked.

Mr. Lavictoire's face lighted up. "Louise?" He turned toward the house and hollered. "Louise! Louise! *Viens ici!*"

Louise appeared barefoot in the doorway. Her father beckoned her with his hand, and she grinned and ran to join them.

Mr. Lavictoire slipped his arm around Louise's thin shoulders, and Gus noticed how his eyes shone when he looked at her. His tough, weathered face cracked a smile that revealed two missing teeth as he spoke to his daughter.

When he finished, Louise turned to Gus's grandfather, and he repeated his offer. Louise listened intently and translated.

This time Mr. Lavictoire's faced looked shocked, as if someone had slapped him.

"Moi?" He put an open hand on his chest, where his threadbare shirt was already soaked with sweat, even though the day was young. Then he looked toward Gus and nodded toward the field. *"Merci. Allons-y."*

"He says, 'Thank you. Let's get going,'" Louise said, and she looked ready to climb aboard the tractor, too.

But the haying wouldn't include Louise. Mr. Lavictoire spoke to her quickly, and Gus was startled to see her eyes fill with tears. Louise never cried—at least she hadn't at the deaths of any of the ducks or when she just about ripped her thumbnail off hammering the stakes into the garden border. Gus thought she was probably about as tough as the steel in that hammer, or just about anything or anyone else around. Without a word, she turned and trudged back to the house.

Gus's grandfather did two passes with Gus clinging to his shoulders to show him the pattern he should follow in haying the field. Then he put the tractor in neutral and climbed down. Gus slipped nervously onto the seat.

"Just do what I told you and follow what I started," Gus's grandfather instructed. "You'll get the hang of it. Holler if you get into trouble."

Gus put the tractor in gear, and it bucked into motion like the racehorses at the fair leaving the starting gate. Grabbing the steering wheel so hard his arms ached, he carefully steered the tractor around the field, following the pattern his grandfather had established. His grandfather stood and watched until he was sure Gus wouldn't do any major damage, and then he went over and lay down under the single apple tree in the side yard. He pulled his hat over his eyes and didn't stir.

According to his grandfather, Gus did in one long day what would have taken Mr. Lavictoire three or four days to do by hand. They stopped once for dinner. Mr. Lavictoire came over and used his hands to mimic eating. He pointed toward the house, smiling through the grime on his face. But Gus's grandmother had figured there'd be little enough for the Lavictoires, so Gus and his grandfather sat in the shade of the tree and ate the sandwiches she had packed for them.

During the afternoon, when the sun seemed stalled overhead, Gus thought the day would never end. Sweat poured into his eyes, his hands were numb, and his head throbbed, both from the noise of the engine and from the fierce concentration it took to follow the undulating contours of the fields. When he looked behind at his work, however, he could hardly take his eyes off the hay that had fallen unbroken behind him in graceful waves like water flowing over a waterfall.

All day, Mr. Lavictoire limped along behind the tractor, using a hayrake to fuss with the endless stream of sweet-smelling hay, spreading it out so it would cure faster. From time to time, Louise appeared at the back door and watched, the longing in her eyes to escape the drudgery of her household chores visible clear across the field.

In the late afternoon, Gus and his grandfather drove the tractor back down the road. Golden light raked across the neat fields of cut hay that now surrounded the Lavictoires' house on three sides. Gus was exhausted but happy. He felt he had done a man's job, even though he was pretty sure that he had gone stone-deaf in the process.

"Why was Mr. Lavictoire following the tractor?" Gus asked his grandfather that night over a late supper.

"Helping the hay to cure quickly and saving his pride," his grandfather said, watching oleo melt in the mashed summer squash on his plate. "There wasn't much else he could do on his own farm to make himself useful today. If he just stood around watching us, he would've felt like a fool. Or a charity case."

"Are we going back to help put the hay in the barn after it

dries?" Gus asked. He had done that once already this season, and he knew that plenty of hot, sweaty work still lay ahead.

"You are, but I'm not," his grandfather said.

"Why not?" Gus asked. He felt good about what he had done. He thought it would be neighborly if his grandfather lent a hand, too.

"Every man's got his pride," his grandfather replied. "I think Mr. Lavictoire will keep most of his if he puts up his own hay, even if it takes his whole family and you, too, to do it."

Gus's grandfather let him sleep in the next two mornings. He said the weather was perfect for curing hay and Mr. Lavictoire was probably just letting the hay dry. On the third morning, though, Gus's grandfather woke him early and sent him over to the Lavictoires' with a lunch his grandmother had packed. The timing was perfect. Mr. Lavictoire was just starting to hitch the dump rake to the horse. He didn't seem surprised to see Gus; he just pointed to the seat and Gus climbed up.

The day was nearly silent and left Gus spent, but he took that golden field of hay and made windrows, those graceful streams of hay that lay like stripes across the fields. The next day, Mr. Lavictoire handed Gus a fork and again, without saying a word, showed Gus how to gather the hay and stack it into tall, round, beehive shapes that his grandfather called tumbles. Only on the third day did Louise and her younger brothers and sisters come out of the house to help bring in the hay. But even then Gus and Louise had few chances to talk. At the end of the day, Gus rode the bike home and fell into bed without waiting for supper. He had acquired enormous respect for how hard his grandfather had worked all those years. His dad had been right: Farming wasn't for the weak. Gus could see how it could break or even kill a man.

A week later, Mrs. Lavictoire had her baby, a boy, named René for his father. Gus learned of the birth from his grandmother. She had picked up the news at the general store from some of her friends who were clucking about this latest Lavictoire mouth to feed.

School resumed, but Gus hardly ever saw Louise, not even for those few precious minutes before and after school. Occasionally, she came to school; often she didn't. When she did, she was looking mighty peaked. Once Gus decided to ride the bike over to see her. As he was checking the tires before he left, his grandmother came out and handed him a small package.

"It's for Louise's mother," she said.

"What is it?" Gus asked. He peeked inside the brown wrapping. Something was white and clean and neatly folded. It smelled of bleach and crisp air and the heat of his grandmother's iron.

"It's nothing. Just a torn sheet," his grandmother said, shaking her hand as if the package were too small to have any significance. "I thought Mrs. Lavictoire could use it for diapers, that's all. Don't make anything of it. I was going to have to tear it into rags anyway."

In late October, Miller's Run held a gigantic scrap drive to collect steel, aluminum, rubber, iron, and copper for the war effort. A man on the radio said the government needed 17 million tons of scrap metal in 1942 on top of the 13 million tons it had already collected. Airplanes and tanks and trucks had to be built for the fighting men, and they could get what they needed only if everyone did his part. Gus's grandfather had been waiting for this.

"Come on, Gus," he said, turning off the radio with all of its news from the Pacific, where the Japanese and the Americans were trading islands like baseball cards in vicious and bloody fights. Together, they headed out to the barn, where Gus was astonished at what his grandfather had collected by rummaging around and by stopping along the roadside whenever he found something that might be salvageable. To begin with, he had fifty or sixty tin cans. He had several metal buckets with holes in them. He had a rusted set of bedsprings and an automobile axle. He had a tractor seat and the old potbellied stove from the parlor. He had a dozen license plates from heaven knows where. Gus helped him load everything into the back of the truck, and they bounced their way into the village.

On the small green at the center of town, a party seemed to be in progress. Elderly men Gus had never seen before were arriving in their trucks from the far corners of Miller's Run. A few came in horse-drawn wagons. Every vehicle was piled high with a rusty assortment of junk that could be salvaged for the war. Someone brought the blade of a shovel, someone else brought fence wire that Gus wished he'd had earlier in the summer, when the ducks were being pests in the garden. One man brought an old Edison phonograph that to

Gus sure seemed a shame to part with, until the man said it didn't work anymore and the army could use the copper wire inside. Added to the growing pile were a watering trough with a hole in it and the wheels from a drag plow, a reel lawn-mower, and a kitchen stove that was nicer than the one in the Lavictoires' house. The pile grew to the height of Gus's chest and covered a space equal to that of a small house. Nobody knew for sure how much it all weighed, but nobody could say Miller's Run wasn't doing its part.

By late afternoon many of the men had begun drifting to-ward home when one of them squinted into the sun and said, "Would you look at that?"

Mr. Lavictoire was driving his nag and wagon into town. The wagon was loaded with half of his front yard—barbed wire, the washing machine, and two or three tubs of the kind, Gus noted, the Lavictoire kids took their baths in. But these must have had holes in them, or why would anyone give them away? Much of the wagon bed was filled with parts from the truck that had died long ago when someone else owned the farm and until today had lain disintegrating in the front yard, like the remains of some long-extinct dinosaur. It was hard to believe the horse could move any slower and still be in motion, but there was no doubt where it was headed.

Mr. Lavictoire pulled up beside the pile of scrap, and Gus was afraid the horse would collapse and die right there. It was a good thing that the horse didn't know yet that he was going to have to climb back up that hill—but at least then the wagon would be empty. Mr. Lavictoire nodded to a few of the men, and they nodded back. He climbed down from his seat, and everyone started unloading the wagon. Nobody said anything.

When the wagon was empty, Mr. Lavictoire climbed onto the seat for the ride home.

An awkward silence followed.

"Merci," Gus said finally to break the awful quiet.

The men on the green, including Gus's grandfather, turned and looked at Gus with astonishment, as if he had been caught speaking in tongues. Gus blushed under their amazed stares.

"You are very much welcome," Mr. Lavictoire said, speaking carefully, as if the surprised men clustered around him were stupid or hard of hearing. Then he started slowly up the hill.

Without Louise or the ducks to keep him company, Gus took to roaming in the colder weather. He would come home from school, put on his barn jacket, and take his grandfather's .30-30 rifle out into the fields or into the woods beyond the fields. He didn't intend to shoot anything, but he knew that he could. He could blow the center out of a target now from fifty yards, and he enjoyed snapping the rifle into place against his shoulder and drawing a bead on a squirrel or a bird, or even every once in a while at dusk on a deer grazing in the fields at the edge of the woods. He was always careful to keep the magazine empty and the barrel pointed down when he was walking, so there weren't any accidents, but he kept a few cartridges in his pockets just in case he found a good rotted log to take practice shots at.

The fields his grandfather had hayed in early fall were rough stubble now. The autumn reds and golds had come and gone in the woods. Most of the trees, except for the oaks, were bare. The oaks, his grandfather had told him, hated to give up to the cold more than the other trees. The stubborn ones, he said, kept some of their leaves clear through the winter, though the leaves themselves were brown and brittle as old paper. Gus was surprised to see a whole world he had never suspected in the trees when their greenery obscured their skeletons—abandoned nests tucked into the crooks of branches, dead trees riddled with holes where woodpeckers had kept busy, even bigger holes where he guessed the owls he listened to at night had spent their time sleeping and raising their young. It had all been here, right under his nose, the whole time.

Geese and ducks were flying overhead now, heading south. At night, Gus could hear the geese honking. Theirs was a mournful song, full of loss and separation and homesickness that sometimes made him think they were singing just for him. During the day, when he heard them crying overhead, he would look up to see long skeins of ducks or geese stretched across the sky, flying in their lopsided chevrons and changing formation like children playing an elaborate game. He didn't know what was going to become of the two ducks on the pond, but he wondered what their reaction was when they heard the sounds far overhead.

"Do you think my ducks can fly?" Gus asked at supper one night. He felt funny calling them "my ducks." If it was possible, he loved them even more than he had the day they hatched, and he was careful to take some tidbit to them every evening, but he knew they were no longer his in the way that his baseball or his deck of playing cards were. The ducks came when he called, but only because they wanted to, not because they depended on him—they could fend for themselves. After everything he had given them, they had no need for him now. But his love hung on as strong and pure as summer sunlight.

"I'm sure they can fly," his grandfather reassured him.

"But they never have," Gus said.

"They've never needed to," his grandfather reasoned. "They've been pretty well taken care of here. I don't suppose they're in any hurry to leave."

Gus kept his eyes open for a sign. Sometimes when he was standing at the edge of the pond watching the ducks, he heard rifles and shotguns being fired as hunters tried to bag some of the autumn bounty. The periodic cracks reverberated in the small bowl where the farm lay and echoed off the hills.

One afternoon, while Gus was out roaming in the woods with his grandfather's .30-30, he heard the report of a rifle closer than usual. He made a wide circle down the tree line to the east of the house and worked his way toward the pond. Staying in the woods, he walked quietly toward the source of the sound, trying to avoid the fragile, noisy leaves that carpeted the forest floor. He walked cautiously, certain that whoever it was could hear his throbbing pulse and short, quick breaths. Suddenly, it came to him all at once that anyone shooting from here could have had only one target in mind.

Without thinking, he slipped six cartridges into the magazine, and snapped the lever forward and back to chamber the first one. His heart was hammering in his throat, which was swollen and cutting off his breath. He remembered killing the raccoon and closing his eyes against how awful it had been. At that time he had not wanted to do what had to be done. He had shot only because his grandfather had insisted, had told him he had to shoot to protect his ducklings. But after a summer of tending them and watching them grow beautiful beyond his ability to describe, he didn't need any egging on. He felt white anger rising in him like gall against anyone who would hurt the two ducks he had left. He walked softly through the woods closer to where the shot had come from and saw through the trees a figure taking aim with a shotgun at the pond.

Very deliberately, Gus raised the rifle to his shoulder and aimed at the figure. "Don't!" he screamed.

The man's gun dropped to the ground. He raised his hands from his sides and turned to face Gus.

Now Gus's heart stopped beating altogether.

Mr. Lavictoire looked toward him, his eyes two dark orbs and his gaunt cheeks as white as one of Gus's grandmother's freshly laundered sheets. Gripped in his hand was one of Gus's ducks. His overalls were wet to the knees where he had waded into the pond to retrieve it. Now, from the relative safety of the woods, he had been taking aim at the last duck with his rusty shotgun.

Gus froze, his finger tight on the trigger. His aim steadied. He tried to think, but he was possessed by anger so intense and painful that it felt as hot and pure as the fire of stars. He remembered his grandfather's admonition never to point a gun at a man unless he was prepared to shoot him, and he gripped the rifle tighter.

Gus didn't know how long they stood there, but he kept his rifle pointed at Mr. Lavictoire's heart and knew that he could hit it. Mr. Lavictoire's wide eyes never left Gus's face, and he held the dead duck in his shaking hand while its blood ran down his sleeve and stained it the color of blueberries.

"Give me the duck," Gus said finally. He braced the rifle butt against his shoulder with his right arm but removed his left hand from the barrel and pointed at the duck.

Mr. Lavictoire glanced at it. He almost seemed surprised to see it dangling from his hand.

"Give it to me!" Gus yelled and started walking toward Mr. Lavictoire, never lowering the rifle.

When they were no more than a few yards apart, Mr. Lavictoire slowly lowered his hand and reached toward Gus. Gus inched forward and took the duck. He tossed it in the leaves behind him and then put his left hand back in position on the barrel. He bobbed the rifle toward Mr. Lavictoire's shotgun, and Mr. Lavictoire reached down and picked it up without taking his eyes off the rifle that was still pointed at his heart. Then Gus motioned with his head toward the woods.

"*Si te plait*," Mr. Lavictoire begged and shook his head. His eyes pleaded, saying everything he could not.

Gus motioned with his head again. Mr. Lavictoire looked

at Gus hard, as if gauging his intent, and then took off running, his bandy legs giving him the awkward gait of a frightened, wounded animal.

Gus held his ground, the rifle raised and pointed at nothing, until his hands ached with the effort of gripping the gun
and he could no longer hear the ebbing sound of Mr.
Lavictoire's boots in the dry leaves. Then he collapsed into
the litter of the wood's floor.

He gulped air while his mind keened and the brittle
leaves beneath his cheek broke like glass into a thousand
shards. He breathed deeply over and over again, as if he were
struggling to build a wall so high the pain that lay beyond it
could never reach him.

When he was finally limp with exhaustion, he sat up and
emptied the magazine of its cartridges. Holding them in one
hand and the rifle in the other, he looked at the ammunition
and turned and heaved it into the woods. Then he knelt beside Roosevelt. He stroked the duck's iridescent head, so
bright against the red and yellow leaves, and studied the dull
black eye that stared lifelessly back, the light already drained
from it. Looking around, he spotted a sturdy stick, and he
began to scrape out a hole in the earth.

After he had buried the duck, he looked around for
stones, which he stacked on top of the grave until he had built
a cairn that he hoped would keep wild animals from scav-
enging. Standing up, he recalled Louise's eulogy at the grave-
side of the unhatched duckling, Babe, early in the summer.
He could not recall the words exactly, but he remembered the
sentiment and could draw on three months of listening to

Louise converse with her family. He decided to do the best he could under the circumstances.

"*Erposez-vous* in peace," Gus said quietly in the thunderous stillness of the woods.

After paying his final respects to Roosevelt, he walked to the edge of the pond, knelt, and called for Candy. "Hey, ducks."

Then he realized there was no use anymore for the plural. Only one duck remained. "Hey, duck," he called in a hoarse whisper, but his voice nonetheless carried across the water.

Candy plied the water determinedly toward him, a flotilla of one on a clear mission, until she could reach the crumbs Gus tossed to her. Unaware that there would be no more competition for food, Candy plucked quickly at them. When he had given her everything he had, she treaded water in front of him, waiting hopefully for more. Finally, discouraged, she swam away.

Looking down through the green water to the mud on the bottom of the pond, Gus could see small brown salamanders with soft yellow bellies paddling among the weeds. But just below the surface of the water, his reflection stared clearly back at him. He was surprised to see his face, to see nearly all of himself as he was then—with his red hair needing one of his grandmother's monthly trims, his limbs long and lanky, but his body heftier and beginning to fill out his jacket in a way it couldn't have four months earlier. In a dozen small ways he looked different from the way he looked in the photographs his mother and father had taken with them to their separate destinations. He was no longer the boy in those photographs. He knew this not just because he could see it but because he could feel it.

For that matter, his mother's and father's experiences had probably changed them, too. He doubted that the individual photographs on his dresser of his mother and father, and the most important image he had—of the three of them together last winter skating on Boston Common, tangible proof that they were indeed a family, even if they had been flung far and wide—truly reflected any of them anymore. He knew they were all—his mother, his father, and himself—being changed by their experiences of the past few months. Hereafter, they would each divide their lives into the days, months, and years before and after the summer of 1942.

―――

"Son, if you have a lick of sense, you'll get your seat in that chair as fast as you can," Gus's grandfather announced as Gus came into the kitchen after washing up. "Your grandmother has prepared a feast for us tonight."

Gus had scrubbed and scrubbed his hands until they were pickled and white, but he still felt as if they were stained with some of the duck's blood. He rubbed them again on his overalls—if his grandmother had seen him do that, she would have made him start washing all over again—but he could not rid them of the warm, slippery feel of the blood.

Gus lowered himself into his chair and looked around: chicken breasts and thighs swimming in thick brown gravy. Mashed potatoes. Green beans. Bright orange squash drizzled with maple syrup. Hot rolls. It nearly made him sick.

They lowered their heads, and Gus's grandfather offered the blessing. "Dear Lord, thank you for our good health and the bounty of our table. Please watch over Gus's mother and father. Keep our fighting men out of harm's way. Amen."

Gus's grandfather dove for the chicken like a lightning bolt from the sky, while his grandmother beamed, well satisfied with her afternoon's work. But as the food was passed around, Gus was hardly able to help himself to any of it. He pushed the mashed potatoes around his plate and avoided the chicken entirely until his grandmother asked him with exasperation, "What's gotten into you, young man? Your appetite off?"

"I'm just not hungry, that's all," Gus said.

"Don't be a fool, boy," Gus's grandfather said, making a small mountain of mashed potatoes. "We're not eating many meals like this these days."

But when Gus looked at the abundance spread before him, he could think only of the Lavictoires' table tonight. It was supposed to look something like this, the lean dark meat of a single wild duck probably tipped with floury gravy and surrounded by a handful of small potatoes, all of it divided among eight hungry mouths. That had been Mr. Lavictoire's plan—to provide something special for his hungry family. Sure, he had killed one of Gus's ducks, but Gus in the pain of the moment had insisted he give it back, even though it was dead and the damage already done. Now the duck lay decaying in the ground, good for nothing, not even a few succulent bites for his best friend.

Gus eventually ate everything at dinner except the

chicken. He said nothing about his encounter in the woods with Mr. Lavictoire. He said only that Candy seemed to be alone now.

"There are a lot of hunters out this time of year. Maybe the same one who took the last duck came back for another," his grandfather said between bites of squash. "I know those ducks are nearly wild now, but they're pretty tame, too. Even for the clumsiest hunter, they'd be an easy supper. I'm sorry, Gus. You've made me proud raising those ducks. It's a shame there's only the one left."

In bed that night, Gus finally let the tears that had been pushing behind his eyes overflow. He wished his grandfather hadn't said anything about that first duck and who might have taken it, because he now understood who had known that the Amslers had gone to the fair that day. He wondered if Louise knew that her father had betrayed her by stalking and killing something she loved and had worked hard to raise, just to put a warm dinner on the table for his family, and he guessed that she didn't. But Mr. Lavictoire's betrayal wasn't because he didn't care about her feelings. That couldn't be true. She was just about the only thing that made her father's face light up. She was more than his right hand. Recalling how Mr. Lavictoire's eyes had glowed with pride the day he called her from the house to translate for him, Gus saw him now in all his despair. Bright, spunky Louise was the opportunity he was never going to get in the foreign country they had chosen for a home. This afternoon, Mr. Lavictoire had betrayed his daughter again to feed his destitute, unlucky family. If

Louise ever found out, Gus wasn't sure she would be able to forgive her father's treachery. With that thought, he suddenly realized that Mr. Lavictoire had not been begging for his life after all, or even for the duck, but for Gus's forgiveness and his silence.

He cried, too, for the duck that had been killed today. He had hatched it and raised it against all odds. He had loved it from the day it wobbled free of its shell looking drowned and helpless, and he had kept it safe—until this afternoon. Under the sheet, his hands shook when he thought about pointing the rifle at Mr. Lavictoire's heart and almost killing a man to protect what he loved. He thought about his father going off to war to kill other men to protect the ones he loved. He wondered how his gentle father could do such a thing, but it was clear from his letters that he was ready to do just that. Gus thought about his own finger on the cold trigger and how war must force men to do terrible things for love. He understood for the first time that although his father would probably come home—had to come home—he would never again be the same.

Chapter Twelve

The next morning, Gus walked into the kitchen and found his grandfather shouting into the telephone's mouthpiece. His grandparents used the big oak telephone so rarely that it mostly hung on the wall like a decoration. His grandfather did not believe the telephone could transmit sound without losing volume over the long wires, so he always shouted to make sure that at least a whisper of his message would be heard at the receiving end.

"Saturday, first thing. I'll see you then," he hollered and hung up.

"What's happening on Saturday?" Gus asked as he took an apple out of the bowl on the table, eyed it for wormholes, and bit into it. Its tartness exploded in his mouth.

"Sit down, Gus. Eat your oatmeal," his grandmother commanded. "You can't go to school on an empty stomach."

Gus wanted to say "The Lavictoires do it all the time," but he knew better, so he only replied, "It won't be empty. I'm eating an apple."

"Don't be cheeky," his grandmother replied. She doled out a small hill of oatmeal, dribbled some maple syrup on it, and splashed it with milk. "Now, sit down and eat, or you'll be late for school."

"We're slaughtering the hog," his grandfather explained. "I heard that Paul Gordon had enlisted as soon as his dad's hay was put up, and I want his help. It's a lot of work to slaughter a hog, and I aim to get it done before Paul leaves. He's coming over first thing Saturday."

Gus waited two days for Louise to come to school to tell her that only Candy survived, but she didn't appear, although Henri and André did. Gus wondered why the truant officer hadn't gone after Louise long before this. If he'd missed as much school as she had, he was fairly certain someone would have come knocking on his grandparents' door. But maybe the town didn't much care if the Lavictoire children got an education. Finally, he wrote her a note saying that he had something important to tell her. When school ended on Thursday, he caught up with her brothers just as they started up the hill toward home, and he pressed the note into Henri's hand.

"Please give it to Louise," he said.

"Okay, Louise," Henri said, and both boys took off running and laughing as if he'd said something hilarious.

Gus was disappointed when he didn't see Louise at school the next day. He had hoped his note would have made her come. When he was supposed to be working on his geometry, he was thinking instead about riding his bike over to the Lavictoire farm after school, but he was afraid of running into Mr. Lavictoire. Whenever he thought of Louise's father, the index finger on his right hand curled instinctively around his pencil, as if it were a cool, metal trigger. Gus had been down to the duck's grave once to think. He squatted beside the small mound of stones and agonized over what to tell Louise. He had lied to her before and been lucky to win back her trust. He did not want to lie to her again. But his anger over the killing of the duck was surely some sort of test of his character. His grandmother had always said that pain shared was twice as easy to bear, but he wasn't sure that wisdom applied in this case.

After school, as he was walking up the road toward home, he was surprised to see Louise leaning against a tree trunk near the fork in the road. Henri and André sprinted over to their sister, and she smiled at them and ruffled their hair and spoke something Gus couldn't hear. The boys turned to look at Gus, broke into broad grins, and scrambled up the road toward home. Gus approached Louise slowly, studying her. Her hair was dull and badly cut. The jacket she wore had been patched until little of the original material remained. It was ridiculously large for her. At least her hands must be warm, since they were hidden deep in the sleeves. Her complexion was sallow, and the dark circles she had under her eyes seemed to be an even deeper shade of purple. But her eyes were as alert as they always were, and she grinned when he reached her.

"Why haven't you been in school? Where have you been?" he asked.

"Helping mama. The baby cries a lot. With the other little ones at home, there's a lot to do." She shrugged.

"Don't you miss school?" he asked. He thought he

would go stir-crazy with only babies to keep him company.

"Yes." She laughed shortly. "I've read all of my books for the whole year already. But what am I supposed to do? Mama has no one else to help her. . . . I can't stay long. What do you want?"

"Just to see you, for one thing," Gus said before he realized what he was saying. He blushed. "Mostly I wanted to tell you that another one of the ducks is gone."

"Candy?" Louise asked quickly.

Gus shook his head.

For a moment, Gus thought she might cry again. Louise, who was as tough as a butternut. If the ducks were anyone's they were his, but Louise had spent enough time with them to make a claim for them, too. Like Gus, she had fed and watered them and cleaned up after them, but she alone had decorated their brooder, given them names, insisted that they receive proper funerals, and laughed when she could get them to march behind her—a waddling parade of preening gossips.

"What happened?"

Gus could read the loss swimming in her eyes, and he considered his answer.

"I don't know," he said finally, committed to his lie. "I went down to the pond the other night to give them some food, and there was only Candy. I've been down every evening since, and she's the only one that comes."

"Maybe it was the same thing that happened to the other one that disappeared." Louise took a big breath and sighed.

"Yeah, probably," Gus agreed. Except this one hadn't ended up in her stomach like the last one, he thought.

"Well, *bonté divine* it wasn't Candy," Louise said. "I couldn't bear losing Candy."

"Me, either," Gus agreed again, thinking how close Candy had come to also being a feast at the Lavictoires' table. He tried to imagine it. Louise practically would have been eating a piece of her own heart—without even knowing it.

"Hey," he said suddenly. "Can you come over tomorrow? Grandpa is slaughtering the hog. We can watch."

"I don't think my mama will let me go," Louise said. "She says there aren't enough hours in the day to get everything done, all the washing and cleaning and cooking. But I'd *like* to come. I've seen hogs slaughtered before. It's awful bloody, but pretty interesting, too."

"Don't ask your mother. Ask your father," Gus said, knowing that Mr. Lavictoire wouldn't dare say no. "And tell him I said hi."

Early the next morning, Gus was up and collecting loads of sticks to add to the woodpile near the hog's pen when he saw Louise trudging up the hill. He'd already made four trips from the woods with his arms full of sticks, each time walking away from the gauzy early light that bathed the house and barn and into the fog that covered everything lower in the valley, including the woods and the pond. As he headed down the road toward the woods, Louise emerged from the fog, her hands shoved deep into her pockets and her head down, like a ghost.

"Louise!" He ran to meet her.

She looked up and grinned.

"I don't know why Papa let me come. Mama said she needed me today, but he told her to let me come," she said, looking both pleased and perplexed.

"Who cares?" he said and turned her back toward the woods. "Help me get firewood."

"First," she said, "I want to see Candy."

The pond was gray and silent when they reached it, lying still and largely hidden, smothered by the blanket of fog.

"Hey, duck," Louise called. "Hey, duck."

Nothing. Gus's heart lurched.

"Hey, duck," Louise called again, and this time they saw Candy paddling toward them. Only when she got close could they hear the small gabbling noise she was making by way of greeting.

"I don't have anything to give her," Gus said, suddenly panicked. He'd always had something for her. He dug deep in his empty pockets.

"That's okay," Louise said. "I brought something for her." She reached into her pocket and brought out half a biscuit, which she proceeded to break into small pieces and toss upon the flat water. Candy ate eagerly, stretching her graceful neck and dipping her bill to dampen each morsel. When the biscuit was gone, Candy continued to wait.

"She is beautiful, isn't she?" Louise said.

Gus looked at all those drab browns blending together, the muted colors meant to make her nearly invisible in the weeds by the pond's edge, the lone extravagance being the white feathers that flanked her tail like painted stripes. He agreed with Louise: Candy was about the most beautiful thing he had ever seen.

"Come on, let's go." He grabbed Louise's sleeve. "I'm supposed to be getting wood for the fire."

They raced into the woods and piled their arms high and then struggled back up the slope, out of the fog, to the hog's pen.

"Well, look who's here!" Gus's grandfather said when he saw Louise. "Haven't seen you around for a while." He bent his head down and continued sharpening a long curved knife on a grindstone.

Paul Gordon was milling about, checking the chain hanging from the pulley on the barn, making sure the huge kettle filled with water was positioned correctly and securely over the fire he'd started an hour earlier. He took the sticks from Gus and Louise's arms and fed them carefully around and on top of the other firewood. The fire coiled around and back in on itself, like a serpent, as it consumed the wood. Paul walked over to the hog pen and picked up his rifle, which was leaning against the barn.

Gus and Louise climbed up on the lowest rail of the fence and rested their arms on the top rail to look at the hog. She had grown enormous over the summer and fall on her diet of kitchen waste, mash, and corn.

"Did you know that pigs can't look up?" Gus said. "They were made for rooting around on the ground, so their eyes can only look straight ahead and down."

"That's terrible," Louise said, sounding both surprised and sorry for the pig.

"Why's that so bad?" Gus asked. "That's where their food is."

"But think of what they never see," Louise responded. "Rainbows. Sunsets. Heaven."

Gus turned to look at her. He was astounded that no one else in Miller's Run could see what the Lavictoires had to offer, even if it was only Louise. Louise alone should have been enough for anybody.

Paul Gordon climbed over the rails and approached the hog with his rifle. The hog had grown so large that she could hardly move, and now she only made the feeblest effort to avoid him.

"Erpose en paix," Louise whispered.

All at once, Gus, too, felt sorry for the hog that had terrified him half the summer and repulsed him the other half with her lazy greed. Paul put the tip of the rifle barrel between her eyes and pulled the trigger. The report was deafening. Too late Gus and Louise put their hands over their ears. The hog collapsed with a *whuff* into the warm bed of manure. Gus stumbled as he stepped down from the fence, turned his head, and threw up.

Paul and Gus's grandfather moved quickly to hook chains to the hog's still-twitching back legs and hoist the carcass up until it hung headfirst toward the ground. Gus's grandfather picked up the long knife he'd been sharpening and thrust it into the hog's throat toward its heart. Gus thought he would be sick again as he watched blood pulse from the wound. Finally, it slowed to a trickle.

"Gus, Louise—come around to the pulley and swing

the hog over the kettle," his grandfather instructed them.

Once the hog was over the kettle, Paul used the hoist to lower it into the simmering water, which turned suddenly pink and frothy. After five minutes, Paul hoisted the scalded hog out.

"You can help with this next part," his grandfather said to Gus and Louise over his shoulder.

Inwardly, Gus groaned. He had decided that watching the slaughter of a hog—even a hog he detested—wasn't quite the entertainment he had expected, and he was ready to suggest they return to the pond if he noticed Louise's interest flagging. But she remained riveted to the business at hand.

Gus's grandfather handed Gus and Louise two scrapers.

"If you can tell me why these are called candlesticks, I'll give you a dime," he told them.

Gus wanted that ten cents, and he studied the scrapers, which, now that he considered them, looked just like candlesticks. "I know," he said. His grandfather laughed and rummaged around in his overall pockets until he'd found a nickel each for Gus and Louise. "If you hadn't figured it out, Louise would have. Now, let me show you how to use them." He borrowed the candlestick from Gus and showed him and Louise how to scrape off the hog bristles.

Gus and Louise began. Louise worked hard, and soon sweat beaded on her forehead. Gus started gingerly, as if the hog could still feel the harsh scraper against her skin, but he gradually managed to separate his thoughts from what he was doing and focus on the job before him. His arm ached by the time his grandfather decided the hog was scraped clean enough to meet his approval.

When the hog was finally cleanly shaven, Gus's grandfather split open its soft belly. Blood and offal cascaded from the wound, and an overwhelming sickening stench that smelled of every rotten egg, every spoiled potato, every moldy piece of bread the hog had ever eaten washed over everyone. Gus's grandfather and Paul reached in and pulled the rest of the entrails out until they lay steaming in a disgusting pile beneath the hog's head.

After that, Paul sawed the hog in half from its tail to its snout with a meat saw while it swung in the cold air. Then he hefted one half onto his shoulder. Gus's grandfather struggled to do likewise, but his old knees weren't up to the weight. Gus knew he should volunteer to help but he couldn't stomach the idea.

"Just leave it there, Mr. Amsler," Paul told him. "I'll get it after Mrs. Amsler has finished up with this one in the kitchen."

From then on, it was only a matter of carving up the roasts and hams, the bacon and loins. Gus's grandmother worked with swift efficiency, separating the meat from the skin and fat with razor-sharp knives and tossing the little that wasn't edible into a big tub by the kitchen table. Gus was shocked to see the intensity with which his elderly grandmother attacked the side of pork, like a starving dog working hard on a bone.

"I have to go now," Louise said when Paul hauled in the other half of the carcass and tossed it with a sickening thud on the kitchen table.

"Have something to eat before you go, child," Gus's grandmother said without looking up. "There's brown bread and beans I've been keeping warm in the oven all morning so I wouldn't have to stop to cook."

Although Gus had lost his appetite hours earlier, Louise tucked into the meal and ate heartily.

"Thank you, ma'am," she said as she stood to go.

Gus was more eager than he would admit to walk Louise out the door, where the fog had lifted, giving way to a sunny but cool day. But she didn't move. Instead, she shifted from one foot to the other and punched her hands deep in her jacket pockets.

"Are you going to be using the head, ma'am?" she finally blurted out.

Gus's grandmother stopped her sawing and looked into the tub, where the hog's head lay in two pieces.

"No, child. I'm not partial to headcheese. Never have been," she said.

"Could I have it?" Louise asked.

"Mercy, yes," Gus's grandmother said. "I should have thought to offer it to you in case your mother could use it. And please take some bacon, too, for your help. Gus, go to the barn and fetch two of the cleanest feedbags you can find."

Louise finally left with the hog's head slung over one shoulder in a feedbag and a slab of bacon in a feedbag dangling from the other. Gus didn't think Louise could have been any happier if someone had given her a green velvet dress with a matching ribbon for her hair. He watched her go, her back straight under her loads and her step triumphant.

"You're not done, young man," Gus's grandmother said from the doorway behind him. "All that meat's got to be soaked in brine and then hung in the smokehouse. Ask your grandfather where he's keeping the corncobs to burn in the smokehouse. Then help me carry the rest of this to the cellar. We've got to bury it in salt in the big barrels down there if we want salt pork this winter."

By the time the Amslers had finished the bloody work of killing the hog and putting up the pork, and Gus's grandfather had paid Paul and wished him well in the army, Gus thought the whole house smelled of death. It was a horrible, acrid stench overhung with something sweet that closed his stomach against even the thought of food, maybe ever eating again. While his grandparents did the last bit of cleanup, Gus went down to the pond and sat in the cold, damp hay stubble to write postcards to his mother and father before the light faded entirely from the sky. Even though his father was going to be a pilot dropping bombs on targets far below, Gus thought about all those gruesome photographs in *Life* and knew that his father was at some time or another going to have to face death close-up. It was inevitable; that just seemed to be what war was all about. He wanted his father to be prepared, so he told him about the killing of the sow and all the blood and what death smelled like because he didn't want his father to be shocked by it when he finally confronted it. And then he told him how much he missed him. To his gentle mother, who had never been hardened by farm life and who could never have witnessed, let alone done, what he had today, he wrote the joke he had been saving all week:

> *Knock-knock.*
> *Who's there?*
> *Pina.*
> *Pina who?*
> *Pina long time since I've seen you.*
>> *Love,*
>> *Your son, Gus*

Chapter Thirteen

Gus was lying on the hooked rug in front of the radio, doing his long division and half listening to a broadcast about how the Allied forces were driving Field Marshall Rommel and his army out of Egypt, when he heard the phone ring in the kitchen. His grandmother answered it and exclaimed "Oh!" loud enough to be heard all over the house. After that, he could hear her talking excitedly. He was mildly curious, but, really, the news on the radio was more interesting. Then he heard her heavy footsteps hurrying down the hall.

"Gus, come quick. Don't waste a minute, boy. It's your mother calling from the sanatorium," she said as she reached the parlor.

Gus was on his feet in a flash and nearly knocked his grandmother over as he sprinted for the phone.

"Mom?" he yelled, as he struggled to grab the earpiece dangling by its cord and raise it to his ear.

"Oh, Gus, it is so good to hear your voice," his mother said quietly, and then Gus could hear her start crying.

"Mom! Mom! What's wrong?" he yelled into the mouth-piece as if, like his grandfather, he put no faith in the telephone to deliver on its grand promises. Out of the corner of his eye, he noticed both his grandparents standing in the kitchen door-way, his grandfather's weathered hand resting on his grand-mother's shoulder. His heart was hammering in his chest and sounded in his ears the way a flock of pigeons sound as they smack the air and all rise together in a rattling cloud.

"Nothing," his mother said more firmly. "Nothing's wrong. In fact, everything's fine. The doctors are releasing me. We're going home. Your father is going to send you train fare."

"Dad, too?" Gus asked, confused.

"No, not your father. But I can go back to our apartment, as long as I take it easy, and that means you can, too. We'll be home for Thanksgiving. I can't believe it," she said. Not just her voice but her relief and her happiness coursed through the phone wires.

"You mean it?" Gus was hopping back and forth from one foot to the other. He wanted to shout and holler. He turned to his grandparents and yelled, "I'm going home!" and one part of his excited, joyful brain noted that his grand-mother clutched her apron to her mouth and his grandfather looked away, back down the hallway.

"I have to go now, Gus," his mother explained. "You know that a long-distance phone call is terribly expensive. But I have one more thing to say."

"What?" Gus could hardly contain the joy in his voice. What more could his mother possibly have to say that would make any difference if they were all okay and he and his mother were going home?

"Knock, knock," she said.

Gus laughed. "Who's there?"

"Gus."

"Gus who?" he asked.

"Gus who I can't wait to see. Goodbye, honey. Make sure you thank your grandparents for everything they've done for you. I can't imagine how we would have managed without them." And then she hung up.

Gus whipped around to tell his grandparents, but his grandmother wasn't in the doorway anymore.

"Where's Grandma?" Gus asked. He wanted to share his news with both of them.

"She's gone to bed. I think she felt a headache coming on," his grandfather explained.

"I'm going home!" Gus blurted out. "Mom's better! She can go home! She wants me to come, too! In time for Thanksgiving!"

"That's all good news," Gus's grandfather agreed. "It's about time you were back together, the way you should be. I have to say, though, it's sure going to be quiet around here without you."

"Oh, Grandpa," Gus said, suddenly afraid that he had hurt his grandfather's feelings. Surely they had never thought his visit was permanent, had they? He'd always been waiting to go home, to his real home and his real life, even if this had turned out to be the best summer and fall of his life—or maybe just the most interesting. He would never have been able to raise ducks in the city. He would never have met Louise. He'd still be hoping that someone would think him old enough to learn how to shoot a rifle, even though he knew there wasn't any place to shoot a rifle in the city. He would still be thinking that vegetables appeared magically in the stores, without giving a thought to the people who had planted, hoed, weeded, and harvested them. No one would ever have trusted him, a boy of thirteen, to watch the night sky and protect millions of sleeping people from German bombers. No one would ever have trusted him to hay a field with a tractor, just like a full-grown man. In Boston there weren't any fields, and nobody needed hay, and anyway, why would anyone even have a tractor in the city? "I didn't mean," he started.

"I know what you meant, Gus," his grandfather said. "And I only meant how much we've enjoyed having you. Sometimes it was more exciting having you around than a whole herd of cows."

They both laughed.

"Come on, son, finish up that arithmetic and head off to bed so you can get some shuteye, if you're not too excited to sleep," his grandfather said and hobbled toward the stairway.

Lying in bed at night now, even with his bedroom window closed tight against the cold, Gus could occasionally hear the wild clamor of ducks and geese migrating overhead. The geese honked, an uninterrupted, haunting rabble of sound without rhythm or key as they crossed the sky. The ducks quacked, sounding less musical and more like a family caught in endless squabbling over who gets the last piece of apple pie. Gus marveled that they could find their way in the pitch-black darkness of a Vermont night.

"Somehow they know exactly where they're headed. I've heard they probably fly according to the stars," his grandfather had said.

"Like Dad?"

In his letters, Gus's father had been telling him about learning to navigate. He had written that they used whatever was at hand to lead their planes to their targets. By daylight, they flew by sight, watching the terrain beneath them and comparing it to their maps. In bad weather, they relied on radio beacons broadcast from below. At night, they let the stars guide them. The stars had names, beautiful names like Orion's Belt, Andromeda, Sirius, and Cassiopeia. In one of his letters, his father had tried to draw a map of the night sky and identify the important constellations, so Gus could look for them, too. It was one more thing Gus could never have done in Boston, where the city lights made you think the sky was just over your head and not some vast twinkling dome too big and far away to imagine.

Gus and his grandfather still huddled on the benches under old blankets in the playhouse on Tuesday nights, looking out the windows and watching the sky, but Gus's grandfather said he couldn't be a spotter much longer. He was too old. He would quit when Gus left to go back to Boston. They'd have to find a younger man to brave the coming weather. But until then, Gus studied his father's pencil drawing whenever he had the chance, trying to memorize it so he could search for those special stars that tied him to his father across millions of miles of space.

Walking to school and in the late afternoons, Gus would hear the ducks and geese flying south, and he would scan the skies to see their skeins overhead. Sometimes he could just see the white underbellies of snow geese flying so high overhead they were little more than pinpricks. Other times, the shifting chevrons would contain so many ducks, he had to strain to count them. Thirty. Forty. He always lost count as the ducks regularly regrouped themselves so no single duck had to take the full brunt of the wind for the entire journey.

Gus never saw or heard the ducks and geese without thinking of Candy. She was still swimming placidly on the pond, as if she had no notion of the approaching winter. Any morning now the pond would be rimmed with ice. The ice might not stay, but it would be a warning. In the afternoons, when he brought her a cracker, she still came when he called. He had no idea if she was too tame to leave or too wild to stay. He didn't even know what he wished she would do.

The first snow arrived the second week in November. No more than a dusting fell in the night, but it coated the landscape. The world turned white and forced everyone to acknowledge what was sure to come.

Louise was waiting for Gus after school the day of the snowfall. She had not been to school for three full weeks. He had wanted so badly to tell her that he was moving back to Boston, but he had not yet screwed up his courage to ride over to the Lavictoires'. Now she stood on the road, just beyond the schoolyard. She wore the same torn canvas jacket that he had seen on her father the day Mr. Lavictoire shot the duck, and it hung on her as if she were the scarecrow in her family's garden. Her fingers weren't even visible beneath the cuffs. Stains the color of blueberries on the side of the jacket made him take a deep breath. Studying her as he walked over, Gus could see the dark circles beneath her eyes. It had been almost two months since she had had her last Vimms. The only sparkle Louise had left was in her eyes, same as the day he had found her in the barn holding one of his duck eggs. Even her grin was different. It didn't beam at him full of wild mischief and unmistakable intelligence; it was still warm, but it looked worn and tired and forced. Her boots, such as they were, were held together with twine, and her overalls were three inches too short.

"We're leaving on Saturday," she said when he approached her.

"What do you mean?" he asked.

"We're moving back to Canada," she explained. "Papa says this place hasn't been good for us. We're going back before winter. Things will be better for us there."

"I'm leaving, too," he told her. "My mom is coming home—to Boston, I mean. I was going to ride over to tell you." His excuse sounded weak even to him. At least she had been thoughtful enough to come and tell him. He'd been so afraid of running into Mr. Lavictoire that he hadn't dare go over, and now Louise probably thought he had been planning on leaving without even telling her or saying goodbye. Her face hardened, as if this was her thought exactly. Gus hung his head.

"Well, then, I guess that's that," she said finally. She turned and started up the hill toward home.

Gus told his grandparents over supper that the Lavictoires were going back to Canada.

"It's probably for the best," his grandmother said, as she passed the turnips. "They never belonged here. As far as everyone around here is concerned, the French should stick to their own up in Canada if they want to speak a different language and pray to the pope. Nobody asked them to come down here to beg and breed like rabbits, pardon me for saying so."

"But nobody even tried to get to know them," Gus protested. "You like Louise, don't you?"

"Yes, I've come to like Louise very much, but she's different. She's not *typical*," his grandmother said.

"How do you know?" Gus asked.

"Some things a person just knows." His grandmother then closed her mouth in a firm line to indicate that she was done with the subject.

"I always wondered why Mr. Lavictoire couldn't improve the place," Gus's grandfather mused aloud. "Granted, it was a poor farm to begin with, but he could have made a go of it. I've seen him work. It wasn't for lack of effort or skill."

"Maybe it was because no one ever gave them a chance. The store wouldn't give them credit, and Mr. Lavictoire couldn't find any help. Nobody would even sell him manure for his fields—and who's so stingy they want more cow poop than they need? Louise said they were *ostracized*." Gus said the word slowly.

"What in sam hill do ostriches have to do with this?" his grandfather asked.

"It's not the bird, Grandpa," Gus corrected him and almost smiled. "It means no one wanted anything to do with them."

"Well, she was right about that, son," Gus's grandfather agreed, "but I figure that's their problem, not ours. They're the ones who came here without being asked, and when they came, they brought more baggage with them than they realized. Nobody around here has liked the Quebecers since long before the Lavictoires showed up. But I'd give you dollars to doughnuts that that little girl makes something of herself," his grandfather said, chewing slowly. "It's too bad, but now, with the war on, Mr. Lavictoire's going to have a hard time even selling the place. Three years of hard work, and he's going home poorer than when he came—and with more mouths to feed."

"When are they leaving?" Gus's grandmother asked.

"Saturday," Gus said, reaching over the turnips to get the potatoes. He hoped his grandmother wouldn't swat his hand for what she called his "boarding-house reach."

"Well, I hope the weather holds off a bit to make their traveling easier," she said, oblivious for once to Gus's lack of manners. She stood up to clear the table.

After the dishes were done, Gus went upstairs to his bedroom and took down the chipped bowl where he kept his money. He had two dollars and forty-six cents, thanks to a banner season of bugs in late summer, after the ducks had been dispatched to the pond, and he had reclaimed his job. He thought of all the things he could buy with that small fortune, but now he counted out the nickels and pennies and put the change on his dresser to take with him to school the next day.

In the morning, he wheeled the bike out of the barn and rode down the hill, bouncing over the ruts that were already freezing up for the long winter. Today he didn't stop at the school, although he could see children huddled around the building, dancing from one foot to the other to keep warm while they waited for the opening bell. Instead, he rode the eight extra miles to town and went to the general store. Inside, while he tried to rub a little feeling into his white, frozen fingers, he studied again the "Uncle Sam Wants You" posters on which a man nearly as gaunt as Mr. Lavictoire pointed his gnarly finger at Gus and made him feel guilty for being thirteen and too young to fight in the war.

Most of the trip back to the school was uphill. By the time he reached it, the children were outside for noon recess. He had missed half the school day and would have to explain why to Mrs. Brewster, so he just kept riding up the hill to his grandparents' house.

"Mercy!" his grandmother said when he walked into the kitchen in the middle of the day. "What are you doing home at this hour?"

"I don't feel good," Gus said, and that wasn't exactly a lie.

She put her cool hand on his forehead.

"You do feel a little warm," she said.

Gus didn't mention the twenty miles, half of them uphill, that he had biked since breakfast. Anybody would be warm.

"You go on upstairs and get into bed," his grandmother

said. "I'll bring you some ginger tea. If your chest is congested, I'll put together a mustard plaster."

Pedaling twenty miles on the bicycle had given Gus an appetite for something more than ginger tea, but it probably wouldn't be wise to make that point. He could live for one afternoon on tea, but he declined the mustard plaster with its turpentine-soaked cloths.

Once he had feeling back in his hands, he spent the rest of the afternoon reading the latest issues of *Life* magazine and *Marvel* comic books. Twice his grandmother came in to check on him. Sick or not, he enjoyed the feel of her hand on his forehead. It reminded him of his mother and the time he had taken to bed with the chickenpox. Then his mother, smelling of soap and lilac toilet water, had swept in and out of his bedroom like an angel of mercy. The thought of it made him so homesick that he actually put his head on the pillow and believed he might be coming down with something. By supper, though, he decided that if he didn't eat, he might just faint.

"I think the boy has his appetite back," his grandfather observed as he watched Gus slather his third piece of bread with strawberry jam.

After school the next day, Gus practically sprinted up the road to his grandparents' house. He breezed past his grandmother and went upstairs and changed into warm clothes. Then he went downstairs to the mudroom and looked over the guns in his grandfather's gun rack. He had practiced all summer and fall on rifles and had never tried the shotgun, which sprayed pellets, but he knew that's what hunters used to get birds. He had watched his grandfather load it, and now he lifted it down off the rack and filled his jacket pockets with birdshot. He knew where the turkeys were. During his rambles in recent weeks, he'd often seen them above the barn, near the tree line where the woods began.

He headed up the hill toward the woods, vaguely aware of the sharp report of other hunters' guns in the distant woods. Sure enough, Gus could hear the wild turkeys before he saw them. A flock of eight was grazing near the trees. They were large, twice as big as Candy, their tail and wing-tip feathers a brighter brown than Candy's, more like the color of chestnuts, their upper wings darker and their bellies a muted red. Their legs were long and sinewy, as if they had been designed for strutting, but their heads were nothing to boast about—bald and bristly. Gus thought that if there were a beauty contest, Candy would win hands down.

He paused as he raised the shotgun and took aim. Don't ever aim a gun at something unless you're willing to kill it, his grandfather had warned him. Now he took a deep breath and held it, considering whether he could do this. Then he squeezed the trigger.

The roar of the blast ricocheting off the hills was deafening. The ringing in his ears drowned out the panic in the turkeys' gobbles, but he watched as half a dozen terrified turkeys took flight. Two lay on the ground. One was still, but the other one thrashed and kicked. Gus swallowed hard. Then he picked it up by its legs and bashed its head against a tree to put it out of its suffering.

Gus staggered down the hill toward the hog pen, carrying the two turkeys by their legs in one hand and a huge armload of wood in the other. The shotgun hung on its strap around his neck and banged into his back with every step. Where he and Louise had helped build a bonfire to scald the hog, he made a smaller fire, over which he suspended a kettle of water. He used an ax to chop off the turkeys' heads and feet so the blood could drain, and when the water boiled, he tossed the carcasses into the kettle. The scalding made it easy to pluck the birds' feathers. Afterward, he used his grandfather's big curved knife to slit the turkeys open from breastbone to tail, and met again the unforgettable stench of death. He pulled the offal out until it made a small steaming pile at his feet. Finally, he gathered corncobs for the smokehouse and lit them. When smoke started curling to the top of the smokehouse, he carried the turkey carcasses up and hung them inside to smoke and dry with the pork roasts and slabs of bacon. By the time he had finished washing up and cleaning and oiling the shotgun, it was dark and his grandmother was calling him in for supper.

"What were you up to this afternoon?" Gus's grandfather asked him over supper. "You seemed pretty busy. I saw you had the shotgun out. What were you after?"

"It's nothing. Just a couple of turkeys," he said. "Something for the Lavictoires on their trip."

"Did you cure them?" his grandmother asked.

"Just like the hog," Gus replied.

"Did you clean the gun?" asked his grandfather.

"Yes, sir," Gus said, grateful that no one asked for more details.

Saturday morning, Gus was up early. He gobbled his break-fast and told his grandparents he was going over to see the Lavictoires. He wanted to say goodbye, and he had a few things to give to Louise.

"I wish them well," Gus's grandmother said as she wiped crumbs off the oilcloth. She looked out the window. "It's gray and cold. That's a tough recipe for traveling."

Before he left, Gus went up to his bedroom and gathered his gifts for Louise and shoved them into his jacket pockets. Then he sorted through his shirts until he found one he had outgrown. He carried it out to the smokehouse and retrieved the two turkeys. The carcasses were surprisingly small. He wrapped them in the shirt and with some difficulty stuffed them inside his jacket. When he climbed on the bike, he looked swollen, as if he had gained twenty pounds in the last two days and all his clothes would have to be replaced.

He was almost too late. The wagon was already loaded, piled skyward with everything the Lavictoires owned, in-cluding the broken sofa and the three-legged table. At the very top, pinched by a rope, lay the stuffed rabbit Gus had won for Louise at the fair. One button eye was missing, and one ear dangled by a thread. It looked as if it had been loved nearly to death.

The little Lavictoire children were swarming around like gnats, chasing after one another and rounding up the small things they wanted to take along. One of them clutched a naked rag doll. Henri and André came racing around the end of the wagon and skidded to a stop in front of Gus with big smiles on their faces. They wore heavy wool sweaters with holes in the elbows. The sweaters weren't nearly warm enough for sitting outside all day on a moving wagon. Mrs. Lavictoire and the baby were nowhere to be seen, and neither was Mr. Lavictoire. The cow stood patiently, tied to the back of the wagon with a rope around her neck, as if she'd done nothing but wait her entire life.

"Wheezie! Wheezie!" André and Henri shouted in unison while they pointed at Gus's huge stomach and laughed.

In a few seconds, Louise appeared in the doorway. She turned and said something Gus couldn't understand and then stepped through the door and crossed what passed for a lawn until she was standing in front of him. She looked at her little brothers laughing themselves silly while they playfully punched each other. She gently slapped them on their heads and grinned at Gus.

"We're leaving as soon as Mama and Papa finish a few chores," she said. She looked at the tower of broken-down belongings on the wagon. "Do you know what I'm going to miss?"

"What?" Gus hoped she might say him but thought she might say "Candy."

"Listening to the radio," she said.

Gus was too surprised to be hurt. "Don't you have radio in Canada?" he asked.

"Yes," Louise said. "But not in English."

"You already know so much," Gus assured her. "My grandfather says you are a spitfire."

"You see?" she asked. "What is a spitfire? How will I ever know now?"

"I brought you something," Gus said with a desperate eagerness to share his gifts.

Reaching into the pocket of his jacket, he pulled out a packet of Vimms vitamins. "These are for you," he said. "I skipped school three days ago and went to town and bought them. There are ninety-six of them, and if you break them in half, like last time, they'll last twice as long. They'll make you twice as alive and vigorous, like they did this summer. And you won't get rickets, either."

He put his hand back into his pocket and pulled out a can of Carnation evaporated milk.

Louise studied the red-and-white can, her brow furrowed in puzzlement.

"I found an advertisement in *Life* magazine," Gus explained. Reaching into his pocket yet again, he retrieved a crumpled scrap of paper and used his other hand to smooth it out against his knee. "Look. It says, 'It gives a girl GO when she EATS her milk.' You'll have pink cheeks and hard muscles, too.

"You just add water," he continued, pointing to the words in the advertisement. "It also says you can partify the milk by making cherry Bavarian cream pie—and here's the recipe. But I figured that even if I could talk Grandma into making the pie, you probably wouldn't be able to take it along, what with everything else you have to carry."

Finally, he reached into his jacket and pulled out a bar of Palmolive soap. "And this," he said, "is supposed to make your skin glow. At least, that's what the advertisement says."

Louise looked at the gifts and grinned again.

"It will be hard to be vigorous and sparkly and glowing and a girl with GO all at the same time," she said. "I might have to lie down sometimes just to rest up."

Now Gus smiled.

"I have something for you, too," she said. "Just in case you came to say goodbye. But it won't make you sparkly." She went and rummaged in a box near the front of the wagon. When she turned back to Gus, she had a feather in one hand and a little jar with colored liquid in it in the other.

"What's that?" Gus asked, studying them.

"It's one of Candy's feathers," Louise explained. "I picked it up in the barn and I sharpened it at the point to make a pen. And this is ink. I made it from sumac, so it's lots more red than blue, but I didn't think you'd mind. It's not the poison sumac. You don't have to worry about it making you sick."

As his eyes grew moist, Gus thought it better not to say anything. He just took the gifts and tried to make his smile look natural. For a moment, he studied the scraggly, tired-looking apple tree in the yard, and thought it said about everything that needed to be said about this farm. Except for Louise. She was the sun that had warmed the grass and turned it into hay and brightened this rundown place. Even without her Vimms, she was the sliver of moon that had sparkled on the roof of this old farmhouse and made it look just like its neighbors during the quiet Vermont summer nights. On a farm that appeared so hopeless it made your heart skip a beat just to look at it, she was a star worthy of a spot in the sky next to Cassiopeia or Andromeda. Although he had sent post cards to his friends in Boston and knew they were waiting for him, he was going to miss Louise very much.

"What's in your coat?" Louise asked. "You look like that big old hog."

"It's something for your father," Gus explained.

They both turned just then and watched Mr. Lavictoire hobble out of the barn with the nag. He saw Gus and stopped. The horse, confused, shook its head and whinnied, impatient to get the whole thing over with. Gus had wondered what this moment would be like. He stood still, considering Mr. Lavictoire. Gus had been afraid that he might cry or that he might start screaming in anger, but he held the man's gaze steadily for several seconds and then nodded. Mr. Lavictoire nodded slowly in return, and then limped on his bandy legs to the wagon and started harnessing the horse.

Mrs. Lavictoire came out of the house carrying the baby. Looking neither right nor left, she climbed onto the wagon seat and called something incomprehensible to the children. They stopped running around and gathered at the wagon. Louise lifted the smaller ones and put them in tight spaces behind the seat. The others scrambled up on the wagon bed and found nooks where they could settle in for the long ride.

"It's time," Louise said. She shoved the Vimms, the soap, and the can of evaporated milk into her jacket pockets.

"Just a second," Gus asked. "Could you translate something for me for your father?"

"Sure," Louise said. She turned toward her father. "Papa, *venez icite.*"

Mr. Lavictoire patted the horse's head with surprising gentleness and walked back to where Gus and Louise were standing. He kept his dark eyes on Gus, and Gus could see him chewing on the inside of his cheek.

Gus unzipped his jacket, and took out the turkeys wrapped in his old shirt.

Both Louise and her father looked surprised.

"Tell him I understand," Gus said, looking at Mr. Lavictoire as he handed him the smoked turkeys. "Tell him I wish you good luck back in Canada. These are to help feed your family along the way."

"Understand what?" Louise asked as she looked from Gus to her father and back again.

"Nothing. . . nothing important," Gus said. "Just tell him, please."

Louise spoke softly to her father as he bent his head down to hear the translation. When she was done, Mr. Lavictoire stood upright and let out a long breath.

"Merci," he said, and stuck out his hand, permanently blackened after a lifetime of hard work.

Gus took it and their hands stayed clasped a second longer after they shook.

"Adieu, Monsier Lavictoire," Gus said, proud to be able to say goodbye to him in his own language. "Good luck. *Bonne chance.*"

"Pareillement," Mr. Lavictoire said, then turned and went to the front of the wagon, where he tucked the smoked turkeys down behind the seat.

"Good luck to you, too," Gus said awkwardly to Louise. "Do you know where you're going?"

"Not exactly," she said quietly. "Back to Canada. Papa says we'll find a place when we get there."

She climbed up into the wagon and settled herself in a small nook between the pots and pans and an oak cupboard with all its glass missing.

"Will you say goodbye to Candy for me?" Louise asked. She rooted around in her pockets and came up with three small crumbs of something. "Give these to her, and tell her I wish her good luck, too."

They left without even bothering to close the front door. Gus stepped back and watched as the wagon clattered down the rutted road. At the rate they were moving, he figured it would take them two days to reach the border, longer to find a new place to settle. Just as Louise's head disappeared down the hill, she looked back at Gus and reached a hand up to clear one eye. Gus had no idea whether she might be crying or just wiping dirt away, but he didn't want there to be any misunderstanding about how he felt about her. He raised a hand of his own and waved vigorously, the way a fairy with her magic wand would dispense sparkle enough to last a lifetime.

When they were out of sight, Gus could feel himself shivering in his jacket. Like his grandmother, he hoped the weather would be kind. In his pocket, he felt the softness of Candy's feather, with all its veins lying smooth and tight. His fingers worked their way gently down to the barbed point. He could possibly use the pen and ink to send Louise a post card sometime. But she hadn't given him an address. People had to stay in one place to have a home and an address, a place where someone could make them grin by sending them a knock-knock joke.

Later, as he was climbing off the bike and putting it away in the barn, Gus became aware of quacking on the pond. This wasn't the nervous quacking of frightened ducks, but it was a commotion. He ran out to the road and looked down at the pond. A half dozen ducks were floating on the water. Four were males, two were females. Curious, he went back to the barn and scraped some old feed off the floor. Then he went down to the water's edge.

"Hey, duck," he called gently. Five of the ducks ignored him. Candy separated herself from the group and swam toward him. He first tossed her Louise's crumbs, and then tossed the grain on the water and watched her gobble it up as the others regarded him with wary interest from a dozen yards away. Candy waited for anything more Gus might have to offer, and when nothing appeared, she swam over and rejoined the group.

"Candy's got company," Gus announced at supper.

"I heard some ducks come in low early this morning," his grandfather said. "I wondered if they were aiming for the pond."

"We usually get some who stop over for a couple of days in the fall," his grandmother said. "They don't stay long."

"They can't," his grandfather said. "If they stay, they'll die. I don't know how they know that, but they do. They'll go as soon as the weather turns clear and cold. Ducks, and geese, too, for that matter, seem to be partial to flying at the head of a steady, cold wind."

"Do you think Candy will leave with them?" Gus asked.

"If she's smart, she will," his grandfather said.

"But this is her home," Gus protested. "She doesn't know where to go. She's never been anyplace else but here."

"The other ducks will teach her how to navigate. She's got to go. It's in her blood," his grandfather said.

"Do you think she'll come back?" Gus persisted. He felt as if something were gripping his heart. He had raised her to be free. He had known from the very beginning that she wasn't like a dog, that she wasn't meant to stay forever. But now the prospect of her leaving tore at him.

"Hard to tell, but, as you say, this is her home. If she goes, she'll know the way back," his grandfather said.

For the next three days, Gus leapt from bed at first light and ran to check the pond. He pleaded with his grandmother to let him stay home from school, but she wouldn't hear of such nonsense. When Mrs. Brewster dismissed the class, he raced up the hill on the bike and ran down to the water's edge, arriving breathless with effort and worry. He never went empty-handed but took a handful of old, spilled grain from the barn floor. Candy always swam over and hovered just beyond his reach, happy to get her ration without competition. The other ducks quickly lost some of their wariness and edged closer, too, hoping to get whatever scraps they could of the grain floating on the water. The weather stayed cold and overcast, as if winter had a mind to settle in early. None of the ducks showed any interest in leaving. They seemed to enjoy the peace of the pond and the friendly handouts.

On the fourth morning, Gus woke to sunlight streaming through his window. In the distance he heard quacking. The sounds were faint through the closed window, but he heard the commotion and ran downstairs. His grandmother was already in the kitchen making oatmeal, but Gus did not stop. Still in his pajamas and barefoot, he raced out the kitchen door and reached the road before he saw the ducks. They were swarming on the water, flocking and then swimming nervously apart, rearing up off their soft bellies and furiously beating the air with their wings like excited dancers. All the while, they gabbled noisily among themselves, quacking and squawking and filling the morning with a painful anxiety.

Without warning, one of the males took wing. It flew in a tight circle over the pond. Two more ducks lifted off briefly to join it before they all settled down on the water again.

Gus watched with his heart pounding. He could not tell Candy's noises from those of any of the other ducks, but she flapped her wings the way they did and rose up on her webbed toes and skimmed across the water, beating it into a white froth behind her.

"Go!" Gus screamed. His voice was unrecognizable to his own ears. "Go!" He flapped his arms and ran several steps forward. "Go, Candy, go!"

Candy stayed on the pond as all the other ducks took turns rising up in short bursts of flight.

Suddenly, Gus sprinted for the house. Tears streaked his

face and the only thing he could hear was a roaring in his ears. He ran back outside, slapping cartridges into the rifle's magazine and then slamming the lever forward and back to chamber the first one.

"Go!" he screamed. His throat felt as if it were ripping. He aimed the gun into the sky and pulled the trigger. The blast exploded in the bowl where the farm lay, echoing off the hills like thunder.

The wild ducks rose with a clatter into the air.

"Go, Candy! Go! *Go!*" Gus screamed again. He slammed the lever on the rifle forward and back again. The spent chamber popped from the magazine and a new one dropped into place. Once more Gus fired into the air, although by now he was sobbing so hard he could barely see the pond.

"She's going, Gus." He felt his grandfather's hand on his shoulder. "She's taking off, son."

Gus wiped the back of his hand across his eyes and watched. Candy was above the pond, her brown wings beating an even tattoo. She lagged behind the wild ducks, but all of them were headed south. His grandmother joined them and they all followed the ducks as they climbed toward the crest of the hill that lay south of the pond. They flew in a ragged group, but as they climbed into the sky, still quacking, they started to sort themselves into formation. For the first time, Gus noticed far to the west a much larger skein of ducks flying in a smart chevron. The ragtag group of ducks from the pond was clearly intent on joining them. Gus and his grandparents stood rooted to the dirt road, transfixed by the drama unfolding in the sky.

Gus watched until the ducks were tiny specks, growing smaller every second. He could still hear them, though—the haunting gabble that was part of the beautiful mystery of their journey. Finally, even that was gone. For a minute, the absolute silence of the farm settled over them, as heavy as one of his grandmother's quilts. Gus realized he was shivering in his pajamas and his feet hurt. Then he felt his grandfather squeeze his shoulder again. When his grandfather spoke, his voice was husky.

"Why don't you come back next summer?" his grandfather said, slipping his own jacket around Gus's shoulders. "Your grandmother and I would love to have you—and Candy—if she comes."

The Saturday before Thanksgiving, Gus went out to the barn and took one last look around. He had put the bicycle in a far corner and covered it with feed sacks to protect it, because with bicycle production down so much, he figured he'd need it when he returned next summer. His grandfather had put the brooder and incubator in another corner and covered them with an old tablecloth. Gus went over and lifted the tablecloth to make sure that the advertisements, now brittle and curling, were still hanging on their nails on the insides of the brooder walls.

In late morning, he climbed into the truck and settled between his grandparents for the ride to White River Junction, where he would get on the train that would take him to North Station in Boston. His mother was going to meet him there, and together they would go back to the apartment on Plympton Street, where his room awaited him. His suitcase was in the back. It was lighter than it had been when he arrived last June because half of his pants and shirts didn't fit anymore. Some of them, he knew, would end up in the bottom of Mr. Thompson's rucksack, but he had packed several things that—unlike shirts and jeans— were irreplaceable. He had folded a sheet of newspaper around the pen Louise had given him to try to keep the fragile feather from tearing, and he had wrapped the little vial of ink in one of his socks. He had retrieved his mother's and father's letters from their hiding place in the barn and had tied them into a tidy bundle with string. Lying flat in the bottom of his suitcase was a copy of Emily Dickinson's poem "'Hope' Is the Thing with Feathers," which his grandmother had copied out for him. It was so short that he almost had it memorized. He understood now what Miss Dickinson meant. Hope had nested in his heart all summer and fall, and kept his spirits up when he started to panic, fearing that he and his mother and his father would never be reunited. All he had to do was start thinking about everything that he'd lost and still might lose, and hope would remind him of all the unexpected things he'd found and of the possibility that everything would turn out okay.

Gus was so excited about going home that he kept squirming around on the seat, until his grandmother finally told him to find a spot he liked and stay put. He looked forward to being in his old school with his old friends. He wondered what life in the city during the war would be like, but he figured he'd find out soon enough. He could recognize a passenger plane in the sky now just from the sound of its engine, but he doubted he'd have much chance to use that information in the city, where the street and building lights often made it hard to see the stars at all, and where the noises of cars and trucks drowned out the faint throbbing of airplanes overhead.

To his surprise, he realized that he would miss his grandmother's vegetables. He felt as if he had spent half the summer on his knees in the garden pulling weeds and killing beetles and worms, but he had to admit that he had eaten royally. He was taking home with him two jars of his grandmother's dilly beans because they were his favorite, and she was sending three jars of strawberry jam home with him for his mother.

They stopped in the village on the way to the train station to run some errands. Gus went into the general store with the half dollar his grandmother had given him to spend on comic books and candy for the ride. Gus's grandfather went into the post office. When he climbed back into the truck, he handed Gus a letter.

"Glad we stopped now rather than on the way home," he said. "It's a letter from your dad."

As the truck bounced along, Gus stuffed the letter in his pocket until he could sit down and read it without his eyes jumping out of his head.

"You take care of yourself and don't grow too big," his grandmother warned him as she gave him a hug on the station platform. Her new raccoon collar, the one made from the fur of the raccoon he'd shot, brushed his cheek, and he realized he was looking down at her. His mother would be surprised at how much he'd grown.

"Remember what I said about next summer," his grandfather said, and squeezed Gus's shoulder with his big weathered hand. "And give our love to your mother. You tell her that if she needs anything, she should let us know."

Gus boarded the train and found a seat by a window. As the train pulled out, he waved. His grandfather nodded once or twice in response and then shoved his hands deep in his jacket pockets, walked to the far end of the platform, and looked up the tracks as if he were expecting another train any minute. His grandmother stood large on the platform, one of her handkerchiefs balled in her hand, her hat slightly askew, and her new raccoon collar framing her face. She waved until the train rounded the curve a quarter of a mile down the track.

As the train passed over the Connecticut River into New Hampshire, Gus remembered the letter in his pocket. It was crumpled from being wadded up, but he took it out and smoothed it on his leg before he opened it. He looked at the address:

> August Amsler III
> Miller's Run,
> Vermont

He slipped his finger under the envelope flap and pulled out the letter.

Lubbock, Texas
November 16, 1942

Dear Gus,

    I hope I'm mailing this letter in time for you to get it before you leave for Boston. If not, I know your grandmother will forward it to you.

    I have my assignment and will be leaving shortly for England. I've been promoted to commander of a bomber crew, which is just what I've been training for.

    Please take good care of your mother. She'll need a lot of help, because she's still weak and requires plenty of rest, so you will have to be the man around the house until I come home.

    Gus, be brave. Nothing is certain in war and it doesn't look as if this one will be over anytime soon, but remember always that I am thinking of you and keep you in my prayers. I'm a good pilot, and I've learned the art of navigation well. However long we may be apart, I will always be able to find my way back home to you.

Love always,
Dad

Acknowledgments

I owe thanks to many people for helping me write this book and place it accurately in the early 1940s. First, I would like to thank my parents, John and Pat Price, for all their love and support throughout the years. In this book, they helped me with a variety of details they recall from their own teenage years at the outbreak of World War II. I would also like to credit my late parents-in-law, Bert and Patsy McCord, who for almost half a century owned a Vermont farm much like the one described here, a place my family and I still think of as paradise on earth. Steve Taylor patiently answered many questions about farm life of the era, from haying to pig slaughtering, and Austin Cleaves filled in the blanks. Peter DeRose and Edward Johnson provided information about the kinds of guns used on Vermont farms sixty years ago, and how to fire them. Tom MacLeay led me to Robert Buck, who told me how pilots navigated at the start of the war, and Charlotte MacLeay read the manuscript and made some corrections, for which I am grateful. Charlotte and Tom also gave me the use of their camp so I could revise in peace, with only loons singing in the background; for that I can't thank them enough. Patsy Fortney introduced me to Collette Gosselin, who, working with my English and Ed Skea's French, managed to reproduce the patois of an uneducated French-Canadian farmer of sixty years ago. Bryan Pfeiffer generously shared his vast knowledge about ducks and birds. The Vermont Studio Center once again gave me an uninterrupted week to devote to writing the first draft. Russell Lee, a government photographer with the Farm Security Administration from 1936 to 1941, took the photograph of an unnamed and impoverished Vermont farm girl foraging in a bucket for food that so haunted me she became one of the characters. Love and indescribable thanks to Katherine Paterson, whose friendship and lunches mean the world to me, and heartfelt thanks to my editor, Virginia Buckley, whose kindness, patience, and wisdom were invaluable in helping to bring this novel to fruition. Jim Armstrong at Clarion copyedited the manuscript and made innumerable good suggestions, and I want to thank him, too. I am grateful to Lia Norton at Clarion for ensuring there were no loose ends. Nancy L. Gallagher, author of *Breeding Better Vermonters: The Eugenics Project in the Green Mountain State,* provided information on Vermont's despicable program of rejecting foreigners and nonwhites in the 1930s and 1940s. Of course, if the book contains any inaccuracies, I alone am responsible for them.

Lastly, love and thanks to my wonderful children, Garrett and Lindsay, who, with their dad and me, raised ducks for five years. The ducks were a wonderful part of those summers, and I thank them for the joy, beauty, and laughter they brought into our lives.